THUGS LIKE US

By

John Carnell

Typeset by Corinna Downes,
Cover and Layout by Mrs Miggins for CFZ Communications
Using Microsoft Word 2000, Microsoft Publisher 2000, Adobe Photoshop CS.

First published in Great Britain by CFZ Press

**CFZ Press
Myrtle Cottage
Woolsery
Bideford
North Devon
EX39 5QR**

ISBN: 978-1-480203-4-64

blog: www.beatthemtodeathwiththeirownshoes.wordpress.com

For
J. J. K & L

God Save The Queen

I was pulling up my trousers when the vision hit. A tingling, paranoid feeling warmed my gut, then crept up the back of my neck, growing in intensity until it hit my frozen brain. I gripped the waist of my jeans tightly as the visible universe fell away. I wish I could tell you what it was I saw that night. But I can't. It was there one second and I was in it and knew it, and understood it, and then, wham! It was gone, just like that, sucked back into my life like a video on rewind.

I steadied myself against the cold, iron vice bolted on the side of the work bench in my neighbour's shed. I looked down at the scabby mattress for Fuzzy Sue, but she'd fled the scene of the crime, worried her old man might catch us.

She was seventeen, I was nearly fifteen.

I stood very, very still, a horrible anxiety washing over me, and all I could think of was the sea. It was coming to reclaim us.

To swallow us all.

I slipped out of the shed and vaulted the chestnut palings into my back yard. 'God Save the Queen' was shredding the already tatty orange curtains of the bedroom I shared with my little brothers. "No future," Mister Rotten screamed over and over, like a shamanic madman. No future for the monarchy, no future for society, no future for me.

Perhaps that's why the whole council estate was getting pissed in the street.

For a moment, I was drawn towards their jubilee. Union Jacks, cider, Woodbines, pale ale, sagging stockings, varicose veins and wonky conga lines. Bollocks. I didn't need them and their poxy street party. I had a tingle in my groin, a realisation in my brain and a pocket full of drugs. What more could a young man want? A future?

Futures were for merchant bankers.

I stepped inside the kitchen, grabbed a slice of Mother's Pride, picked up my leather from the floor and headed out across the dark, lurking gardens before anyone could catch me.

God save the fucking Queen!

I hope she had a lifeboat, because she was going down with the rest of us.

Smash It Up

The Artillery was our regular and it was heaving that night. I was meeting Singe and Bill in the saloon bar. Why did they call it that? I'd seen a few fights in there, but none of them Western style. Most of them were glass-in-the-face style. No style. Welcome to Broadgate.

The Stranglers thumped their way through 'Peaches' and everyone was going up and down. They'd got them going, up and down. Familiar faces were everywhere. Flea, Leech, Jefferys, Spud, Mad Mick the Biker, who wasn't mad, unless you call doing a wheelie up the high street on a Kwaker 250 a sign of mental instability. They all jostled each other for space at the tiny, beer-sodden bar. I walked in unnoticed by the landlord and took my place amongst the rabble.

"Alright Jim," said Leach, going off like a faulty machine gun. "It's my birthday. Going to a party. Everyone's gonna be there. You. Spud. Flea. Me. Wanna come. Want some speed?" He showed me the handful of slimming pills he'd nicked from his fat sister. "Tombstones. Two will do ya. Four will keep your teeth gnashing all night!"

"Nah. I've got some Erics."

Leech's pinned little eyes widened.

"Erics! Wanna sell some?"

I smiled and shook my head. The sleeping pills I'd conned from Doctor Do-Little were getting quite a reputation. "Can't sleep, Doc. Worried about my exams, my mum, the world pushing itself to the brink of nuclear Armageddon." That's what I said to him. Then, he'd looked over the rims of his half-spectacles and wrote out a prescription for my half-lies. Ativan, small blue pills, each cocooned in its own plastic capsule. Three pills and a few pints of lager was enough to push my head to the brink of mental apocalypse. Tonight we were gonna do four.

"Be like that then," said Leech and talked his way back into the crowd. "Going to see The Stranglers next week. Want any speed. Alright Sally!" I didn't care much. He was becoming a wanker. A spouting speed freak. He was alright a couple of years ago. Fat-faced, full of funny sayings. A laugh. But he was seventeen now, and sort of grown up. His life had whizzed by. Drugs. What a waste!

Singe and I were different. We were still bang there. On the case. Righteous boys on a mission. Our pills weren't for recreation, or for sale, they were for liberation. Our motorbike for the great escape.

Skint as usual, I lurked in the corner, beneath the stairs and waited. Singe was late. As usual. Probably wrapped his bike round another lamppost. He was good at that. Great at high speeds in a straight line, crap on corners. Maybe he was going slower on his new bike. A brand new Yammy RD 250. I first saw it parked outside his old man's, covered in seagulls' shit. "Singe," I said, all grossed, "what the fuck is that?"

He just looked at me and smiled. "It's a sign," he said in his usual irreverent tone, "a sign from cod." He was a funny bastard. It wasn't what he said, just the way he said it, raising his hands, beseeching some big supernatural fish in the sky.

The saloon bar door bashed open and in he walked, at last, wearing his ripped jeans and faded black leather. He took off his skid-lid, slapped his gloves inside and spiked up his fine blond hair with his thin fingers. Without looking to see if I was there or not, he ordered two pints of Hurlimans from the corpse behind the bar - the landlady, Penny.

"How's Penny today?"

"Bit under the weather, Y'know."

Singe said something cheeky, it doesn't matter what, could have been anything. Penny's reaction to cheeky was always the same. She feigned indignation and then burst into a mousey laugh, squeaking until the phlegm rose up, high enough in her throat to cough her quiet.

Time for another cigarette.

I hoped Singe would bring the drinks quickly. I didn't want to watch her drowning.

"Alright Jimmy," he squealed handing over my pint. Expectation rippled his rock pool eyes. "Did ya get 'em?"

I reached into the pocket of my leather. Out came a shroud of carefully wrapped bog roll. Slowly, delicately, I exhumed the tablets from their paper tomb, like valuable, ancient artifacts. Singe grabbed both of my arms and grinned manically.

"Erics!" He hissed.

"Sykes!" I replied.

Hattie Jacques would have been proud for her partner, I'm sure. Not many seventies comedy actors got a street drug named after them. These Ativan nearly ended up as plain old 'Sykes' but Erics was more incongruous and appealed to our twisted sense of humour. Plus you had the safety element thrown in for good measure. No parent would ever guess their offspring was abusing a prescribed medication called 'Erics'. It didn't sound remotely like a drug. Drugs all had cool names like smack, powder, acid, puff, blues, coke... and now, in our small circle of freaks, Erics had joined the list. Fresh from the clinical trials conducted on yours truly.

"Four each, yeah?" said Singe, reverently.

"Yeah. Four." I dared. "And two for Bill."

Singe took his tablets and downed the tiny uxbs, lighting the fuses with lager. He squared up to me, adopting a farcical macho pose, chest out, brows furrowed and lips pursed tightly across his teeth. I zoomed into his face for the close-up. His timing was spot on. The juke box was just changing tracks.

"Tonight," he screamed, "we're gonna do the ton."

The bar paused to notice us. I cracked up, as much at their blank faces as the joke. Nobody knew what the fuck we were on about. As soon as they saw it was just us, pissing about as usual, they went back to their business. The juke box started playing some Black Sabbath track, courtesy of Mad Mick and the moment was gone. Lost in our Saturday Night Fever. Five minutes later and I was still laughing. Jokes don't do well when you have to explain them, so I won't bother. You had to be there. One night, when you're up late, drunk, stoned, speeding whatever, watching telly, you'll see this classic zombie biker film and get it.

I don't remember much else about that night. Except Bill joined too late to stop us. By the time he'd swallowed his share, we were already gone. I can remember leaving the Artillery. With Bill chasing. We ran screaming into the wind blowing in off the North Sea, down towards the centre of town, throwing milk bottles behind us as we went. But that was it.

Blank.

Except for the wind.

I'll never forget that wind.

It was coming out of the blackness beyond the cliff top, hitting me full in the face. Warm. Salty. Gulls rode its updraft, laughing in and out of the port's floodlights. It was playful today, but I knew it could easily match my malevolence, blow for blow. No problem. And it was only the messenger. The real power moved slowly beneath it, through timeless tide, deep below the surface. Some sort of race memory crawling, squirming, serpentine.

The karmic current, rising.

The sea.

I'm Alive

It wasn't until I woke up the next morning, that I realised I should have been dead. My head was pounding so hard I was able to detach myself from it on every beat. Pain, freedom, pain, freedom, pain, pain, pain.

The bed was a swamp. I'd pissed it. But at least it was still warm. I wrapped the sodden, grey army blanket around me and tried to sink back into oblivion, but oblivion was for the dead dead. I was only the living dead.

Stumbling down the staircase, I gripped the orange banister hard. I noticed my hands. What had I done to my hands? I looked at the delta of dried blood that had flowed from swollen hills of my knuckles. It was a horrible, black red, dead red. A flaky, ancient puzzle, written in blood. I tried hard to remember what it meant, but it was transcribed in a foreign language, from as far away as last night.

It must have been a good night.

I crept into the front room. Thank fuck nobody was in. Mum was round the market with my little brothers and Dad was probably... down the pub? Our little Jack Russell sat in its basket in front of the unlit fire and looked at me with its one eye. One sad little eye. Not a glint of expectation. No food, no fire, no friendliness, not from me. It knew. I gave it a pat on the head and promised I'd feed it later. Its tail flickered slightly, hopefully, and then gave up.

The kitchen floor was cold. The bare, broken lino sent a shiver through my numbness. But the air was warm. Sunday roast was already cooking. The sickly smell of lamb seeped into my nostrils and sunk to the pit of my stomach. I heaved. Nothing. I heaved again. This time my head was down, kissing porcelain. I swore to God I would never do it again. Just get the demon out of me. Acid bile burnt through my eyeballs as I wretched again and again. "I'm sorry, I'm sorry," I whimpered repeatedly. I knew I had done something terrible. But what? Getting drunk was hardly a crime, everyone got drunk. At least everyone I knew. No, this had to be much worse. I slumped onto the toilet floor and flushed away the bitterness. My breathing eased and slowly the feeling crept back over my sweaty skin.

I felt my face. It hurt. A lot.

On my forehead was a small lump, topped with something crispy. I tried to pick it. Hot, runny agony flooded the spot.

I stumbled up from the floor to look in the mirror.

Two inch gash. "How the..."

I tried to pull my memory back, but it refused to return from the shit bin of my brain.

Singe would know.

I dressed from last night's wardrobe scattered around the bedroom floor. A couple of holes into lacing my Docs, I looked for my leather. Nowhere.

"Shit."

I found it hanging on the line in the back garden. It stank of vinegar.

Heave-ho again! Puke splattered onto the pavement.

Singe had better know.

I smelt like a fucking gherkin!

So Messed Up

Singe's real name was Alan, Alan Selsey, but Singe suited him much better. We called him that because, once, we burnt most of his hair off. We'd set fire to a railway shack and Bill, the third member of our 'revolutionary gang' went running back into the building to stamp out the paraffin-soaked rags.

Waste of time.

Most of it had already taken. Flames rose. But Bill being Bill, he started to kick the flaming rags out of the door - just as Singe went in to stop him.

Whoosh! Singe was soon wearing a flaming turban.

The rag was off in seconds but that didn't stop him dancing. What cracked us up even more was his hair. He went in - shoulder length. Came out - singed to a short-back-and-one-side. Even Bill let up and took the piss. Which is hard to do when you've got no breath from being chased along the railway track by the Old Bill. From that day on, thanks to his baptism of un-holy fire, Alan was reborn as Singe.

His house was up on the higher ground of the East Cliff, a couple of streets of terraced boxes from St. Georges Church, which towered above Broadgate like the wreckage of some stone-age spaceship that had crash-landed. Grey, cold and unusable. Its occupants had long since given up the struggle to survive on our 'heathen' Earth. I walked past, stooping slightly, ready to run if any remaining alien missionaries should crack open the door and chase me with their ancient message of salvation.

The street opened out into the red brick and green privet of Walton Road. Singe's street. Now I would find out what the fuck happened last night.

I checked over the back for signs of his old man. None. The car was gone and the empty garage, open. I belted on the front door. No answer. Singe was still in his sleeping pit.

I opened the letter box and shouted. Luckily he had the room at the front of the house, downstairs. The door opened and there stood the fire messiah, dampened in the dark hall.

"Oh, Jimmy, it's you."

"Who was you expecting?"

"Dunno. Old Bill knowing my luck."

He had a habit of using that phrase, 'Knowing my luck.'

I followed him back down the hallway to his pit.

"Stick the kettle on mate," he said, disappearing through the bedroom door.

I went into the neat little kitchen and waited.

"What happened last night?" I said, searching the cupboards for biscuits. His old man always had a stash.

Singe grunted, stumbling from the bedroom like he'd just been stabbed in the back. "Urggg. Shit!"

"What? What?" He came towards me, his left hand held before him like some sort of cack-merchant.

"SHIT!" He gurgled. "Is it? Is it?"

His hand was practically in my face. Fingertips stained a rich, dark brown. Fingernails encrusted.

"Get away you shit fucker!" I pushed him back. My foot booted into his gut.

"Alright. Alright," he said calmly, turning to show me his back. "Check me." From his shoulder blades, down to his waist he was covered in thick brown crud. "You dorty basterd," I teased, impersonating his Irish mother, badly.

"It can't be…" he sniveled as he sniffed gingerly at his fingers. I started screaming. "You dorty, dorty basterd."

Chased by my taunts he disappeared quickly into his bedroom. A moment later he called out. "Jimmy, come here and see this." There was urgency in his voice, like he'd made an amazing discovery. I stepped cautiously into his doorway to find him with the brown stuff spread over both hands, rushing towards me like some shit-eating zombie. I tried to jink, but he jumped me and started to rub sticky all over my cheeks.

It wasn't even funny.

I pushed him away, drawing back my fist. A huge smile cracked his ice face. He ripped back his quilt like a magician revealing the severed head of his once pretty assistant. Her remains were the mangled wrapper and the sludge stain of a half pound bar of Dairy Milk chocolate, melted into his sheets.

He sank down onto the sweet-messed bed.

"I remember feeling hungry, when I came in. I went to the fridge and..." Singe fixed me, a twinkle in his bloodshot eyes. "I must have loved it so much that I took it to bed."

His impression of a dormouse curling up around a giant chocolate bar started me laughing again. I had to hold it back. My head was throbbing like a broken sub-woofer. A wire had come loose somewhere and was poking the inside of my brain.

Singe threw the mangled wrapper to me and went for a shower.

Cheers. Why not? There were still two whole squares left to balance my blood sugar. As I munched, I looked at my knuckles again. Dried blood, bruising. I marched the short distance to the toilet.

"What happened to my fists?"

"Windows. At the station," he shouted back above the pissing shower. "You punched through the reinforced glass."

"Shit. What was we doing at the station?"

"Smashing windows."

Singe came out of the bathroom, leaving the shower running. "Have one. You stink."

Smoke. Blood. Vinegar. Lamb... and now, Chocolate.

I rushed into the bog and threw up again.

The front door knocked. Singed checked through the curtains then let Bill in. "Is your dad in?" Singe shook his head. He looked down the corridor at me, wiping the spit from my lips and barged in. "You fucking psychos."

"What?!?" I was not in the mood for one of his lectures. He slapped Singe playfully. "I'm never taking anything you two give me again."

"We only smashed a few windows." I said in my defense.

"With your head?" Bill stepped towards me and tried to touch the lump on my forehead. "Fucking looney."

"I don't remember." I snapped, pushing his hand away. Bill's face crinkled around his fat nose. "God, you stink of vinegar."

"Must have been the pickled egg fight we had," said Singe pulling on some fresh jeans. "Outside The Royal."

I looked at Bill for confirmation.

Yep. We'd done it.

"Pickled egg fight?"

"You just marched into the chip shop and told the bird behind the counter you wanted pickled eggs. She asked how many, you said 'this many' and walked out with the jar."

A memory flashback. Singe charging and wrestling me to the floor. A vinegar flood. The jar flying. The acidic crunch as it smashes into the road. Running.

"That was after we got chased out of the Royal," said Bill wagging his finger at me, accusingly.

I stared dumbly.

"The fire extinguisher!" Singe screamed.

Me. Not a clue.

"You set one off and sprayed Oily Harry in the face. He was sitting at the bar with his girlfriend."

"Oily Harry?" I mumbled. Oily Harry. Local villain. Rent-a-Riot. Slapped-over hair. Major bastard. "Shit."

"Yeah, shit alright!" huffed Bill. "Right in the eyes. He was just about to lump you, when I jumped on his back. Knocked him over. The barman chased us out with a baseball bat."

"D'ya think Harry will recognise us?" asked Singe meekly.

"Nah. He was stumbling around, half blind, thanks to extinguisher boy!"

Bill's face let up and he smiled.

Reluctantly.

"So how did we end up at the station?"

"You don't remember the biff chariot?"

We both stared blankly.

"The moped?"

Again, Bill drew a blank. He shook his head slowly, reproachfully narrowing his eyes. "I need a bloody drink."

Drowning Men

The Rising Sun had run aground on a small hill in the centre of town. Like a beached whale, it smelt of decay. The only noteworthy things about this pub were the old, upright piano in the corner and the way the soles of my Dr. Martens stuck to the malt-sodden floor, rasping sickly as I marched across the public bar.

We took our drinks and settled into a corner by the piano. The nicotine stained walls and ceilings, were ready to preserve us, like flies in amber.

Like the regulars.

We sipped, then gulped the crystal gold Hurlimans from our glasses. The alcohol stuck to our blood and towed us back into the bittersweet river of intoxication.

Bill was first to pick up the story.

"After the pickled egg fight, I managed to drag you up the high street and stop you throwing each other through the shop windows..."

Singe glared at me playfully, "You swung me round and I flew into Boots' window. I rebounded like I was made of rubber."

I shook my head. No recollection. Nothing.

"The Old Bill drove towards the chip shop and I steered you through Birdcage Alley," Bill continued. "We ran until we got to The Holly. That's where you did the biff chariot."

The Holly was another shit pub at the bottom of a hill beneath the estate where I lived. From the Prestwell, all sorts of misfits rolled down to its doors and crawled home after the lock-ins, pissed, singing, fucking and fighting, happy for another weekend. But this night the pub was closed. It was a national holiday and most people were either inside watching the TV, or laying in the debris of their street party, supping the dregs of their party sevens, while God was out saving the Queen.

"They wouldn't open up, so you broke into a blue biff chariot. You couldn't get it started, so silly bollocks here," Bill poked a finger at Singe, "silly bollocks told you to take the handbrake off and tried to push you down the hill."

Singe wank-shitted his beer all over the table. Cackled lager bubbled from his nose.

"We were gonna drive it through the doors into the bar, wind down the window and casually ask for a couple of pints!"

I suddenly remembered the light in the porch of the house. The sad silhouette of a man in a wheelchair waving a stick or crutch at us.

I couldn't believe we'd been such bastards.

Singe started to mimic the paraplegic, threatening me with an imaginary stick. "Get off my car you... I'm calling the police!"

I looked at Bill. His eyes confirmed it. It was all true. He was trying his hardest to be pissed off at us, hiding his lips behind his tipping pint, but his eyes shone with the buzz. He slapped down his empty pint glass and sighed helplessly.

"After that you went mental at the station, smashing the windows with your fucking head."

Singe and I stared at each other in silent awe.

This was the best night, ever. We'd gone right to the edge, chasing reason like a terrified chicken in front of us.

"That's when I fucked off home," snapped Bill, "you were talking about nicking a bike and driving it over the cliff." Singe grabbed me with both hands and screamed in my face.

"The moped, do you remember the moped?"

"What bloody moped?" said Bill.

"The one we were going to drive over the cliff."

Silence accused us. Nobody spoke in our defense. We were guilty as charged.

A trickle, then a gush, then a flood of memory. I saw us pushing the Puch Maxi along the road, Singe peddling like mad, trying to start it, swaying through the sickly pools of street light, me tumbling behind, clown-like over the midnight tarmac. The bike started, but it kept on dying. By the end of the road, we gave up and cut down an alley to the Old Park. Here we crashed, dumping the bike in the long grass and bracken, before settling down to a fire, lit with the dregs from its fuel tank. I even had the sense to cut across the gardens to get some blankets from home. Under army surplus cover, we fell unconscious by the roaring yellow glow.

Singe took centre stage to bring the tale to its theatrical end.

"I was woken up about four in the morning, next to a dead fire, with two coppers standing over me." His eyes sparkled as he recaptured the moment from that darkest hour.

"I thought I was dreaming. The coppers were shrouded in, like, mist or something. They said 'got any breakfast' trying to be funny. Then I looked down at my blanket. It was on fire."

Bill looked at me accusingly.

Again.

"Yeah, I woke up earlier, I must have rolled onto the fire. My blanket was alight, so I just got up and went home."

"And put the blanket on me?" Singe's face was all mock-shock.

"I thought you looked cold."

The moment was perfect and broke over all three of us, a torrent of howling. Too much for the landlord. We were making him nervous. His smoked-filled, vein-popping, artery-clogged, eyeballing told us we weren't getting another drink. Singe got up and put some money in the juke box. We listened quietly as the old needle crackled across the scratched vinyl. Anticipating. What sounds could a shit pub like this play for us?

"There is a house in New Orleans..."

The Animals.

"It's called the Rising Sun..."

I rose before my audience and begun playing the piano with both fists. A half-finished pint washed over me, as my head joined in with my hands, thumping the keyboard.

"It's been the ruin, of many a poor boy... my God, I know, I'm one."

Then, lifted magically by my collar, the piano keys still clanking beneath my flailing boot, Bill dragged me from the semi-digested corpse of The Rising

Sun, into the painful daylight and beyond, into the blinding, Salvation Army-soaked streets of Broadgate.

No Future? Bollocks! We were top billing. The sea could come and wash everything away. What did we care? We'd already started.

Fuck Mother Nature.

Her bastard sons were out to play.

No Time To Be Twenty One

I woke slowly, cock in hand, aching for a piss. Looking through the gap in the new purple rags that hung on the curtain wire, I could see from the empty Green outside that it was Sunday.

One whole year on from the Jubilee, but still Sunday.

The tide on slack.

Neap.

I buried myself under the lumpy quilt, hoping for a quick death. But nothing happened quickly on the day of rest. As long as I could remember, I'd always hated the Sabbath. The church bells, the baths for school on Monday. The inconvenience of roast dinner round the shitty fold-down table. And when I was much younger, Sunday School.

"Jesus loves you," spat Mrs. Terrell, with her compliant-eyed boys, sitting cross-legged on the soft carpet in the living room of their neat semi. She was overflowing with love for those that listened, without question, without fidgeting, without staring into the awesome blue sky outside. We only went because summer was coming and we knew there'd be a free camping trip to Sussex. My big sister Debbie told me not to mention the trip. Mrs. Terrell was quick to spot 'deceivers'. So I went. I sat, for four Sundays in a row, listening to 'stories' from the Bible that washed over me, leaving nothing but a thin tide-line of guilt somewhere around my ankles. Then, miraculously, Mrs. Terrell called us back and delivered the good news - we had passed the test and were going to camp. Hallelujah!

The summer camp was great. I went fishing and hiking with Mr. Terrell and helped him with the BBQ. My sister jumped from the van without shoes on and trod in a cow pat. The evenings were spent sitting around a campfire singing kum-bah-yah, which wasn't bad, as it made no sense to any of us. Mr. Terrell's folksy good nature was always tempered by his wife's warnings of 'unrighteousness' and God's wrath that seemed to follow just about everything, especially our bedtime farting and hysteria.

Mrs. Terrell saved her own personal wrath for me, on the way home. She called me 'evil', for singing a Suzi Quatro song. I should've ignored her and carried on entertaining the other lost souls from the Prestwell with my rendition of '48 Crash'. Suzi was about as dangerous to my soul as Starsky and Hutch were to crime on the streets of Bay City. But, I'd never felt fire like that before, her eyes burning deep into my soul with the wrath of God. An angry conflagration, wanting to consume the mistakes he'd made. In this case, me. A ten-year-old boy with a pre-pubescent crush on a leather-clad glam rocker.

What a fucking sinner.

I sat in silence the rest of the way home, glancing from time to time at my ghost-like reflection in the mini bus window, terrified of glimpsing the devil she'd so clearly seen in me. But all I saw was a blond-haired, blue-eyed boy, terrified by his own innocence.

Sunday now belonged to the Terrells. They were welcome to it. But it was still my own personal hell. Perpetual afternoon.

I looked at the tinny alarm clock on the windowsill, two o'clock. I wasn't surprised. Even when I was younger, there wasn't ever any Sunday morning. I'd try to make it happen. Up with the birds. Rush downstairs, shovel in cornflakes, jump over the back garden fences. Knocking doors. If my mates weren't allowed out to play, I'd call on anyone in the street, even the Houghtons! Pikey tramps. But, no sooner had I found someone to play with and somewhere to go, to start a fire, melt some milk crates, I'd be called in.

Time for Sunday dinner.

Time for baths.

All three of us younger brothers in the same tiny enamel boat, stinging shampoo and freezing cold water warmed by pans of hot from the cooker. Carried over Dad's shoulder, wrapped in a frayed towel, we'd be dumped in front of the fire to dry. Three boys pushing and shoving, bending the fireguard to get nearer to the acrid coal flames. Always the 'Top Twenty' on the radio. Always desperate for it not to get to Number One because, 'Sing Something Simple' followed, meaning bedtime had come. And bedtime always meant one thing.

Nightmares.

Nobody would hurt me, beat me, abuse me, but as my soft mind dented the hard, feather-caked pillows, and I slid into unwilling sleep, I'd become the prey, the hunted, the target for an army of chasing monsters.

Sunday seemed to mimic my silent screams with its scary repose.

I came downstairs quietly and looked around the tiny living room. My mum lay asleep on the sofa. Her scarred polyester dressing gown, melted by the cooker's uneven flame, wrapped around her. Her face even tired in rest. In her pocket, the crumpled paper bag of 'smoking sweets'. Sherbet Lemons. She made a quarter ounce last all week. One with her evening cigarette. Hardly worth stealing from her - they always had a second skin of sticky paper and pocket fur.

There she slept, seven-kid tired. Like some 'resting' film star in a run-down trailer.

Her good looks had not faded, rather they'd been scoured from her high cheek bones and prominent jaw line by the daily grind. She'd danced her younger days away on stage, being glamorous and vulnerable, looking for that handsome man to sweep her off her feet and fill the gap her daddy left in her heart when he fucked off. Someone to take care of her and make her feel special again. But all she got was someone like her - a damaged child.

He sat opposite, next to the fire, on his throne, nodding off as he read his book. Imperious ruler of the front room kingdom. Dinner plate on the small table beside him, empty of everything but gravy. But even that had to be left, untouched. He was saving it. He would snap at anyone who tried to remove it. Only he could decide if it needed cleaning with a slice of bread or not.

Patch, our one-eyed dog, was curled up by the fire, eyebrows twitching over both eyeball and hollow socket. Dreaming of what?

I took a piss and grabbed my airgun from the cupboard under the stairs and tried to leave unnoticed.

"Where you going?" spoke Dad, without opening his eyes.

"Out."

"Had your dinner?"

"I'll have it when I come back."

The door shut on some further grumblings about washing up and I was out, walking up the street, past the rows of identical houses on our estate. Nobody was out, apart from a gang of three mongrels looking for something to shag. Nobody was coming out.

It was Sunday.

Number seven. Joe Doyle. Having his dinner. Number nine. Colin Oldman. Catalogue kid. Flicking through the glossy pages looking for his next style. Number eleven. The Scuttons. Tramps. Wouldn't call for them. They rode the Chumley bus to school in the morning, faces pressed against the window.

Pretty vacant.

Across the road, even numbers. Six. The Blakelocks. Darren. Fat-shit-dog-shagger. Avoid at all costs. Number twelve. The Carvers. Jamie, always out running errands for his mum. She was a prozzy, selling it down the harbour. Number twenty four. The other Oldmans. Not related to Colin, but he still had sex with their younger sister and got done. Johnny Oldman was about my age, a nasty bastard. Always playing with knives. His big brother Brian was already in prison for the same.

Back to the odds. Number nineteen, the Houghtons. Mikey and Troy. Travellers who'd stopped travelling some time ago. They didn't give a shit. Mikey was a top laugh, mad as his boss-eyed whippet. But they were always out, totting or rabbiting.

Next door to them lived their 'cousins' the Sanders. Even worse. Six-fingered banjo-playing, police-fighting fuckwits. I didn't play with none of them. Then right at the top of the street, old Revo. Drink-stealing, bike-smashing loony who lived next door to my eldest brother's mate, Beanie. Reggae-loving boot-boy extraordinaire.

Revo was probably in hospital. Beanie was definitely in, his bedroom windows opened wide, some heavy dub throbbing through the curtains. He shouted some playful abuse as I passed. His music went down and he called me back.

"When's Martin back?"

"Dunno."

"Tell 'im to come up and see me."

I gave him the OK sign and left him, his giant frame wedged in the window, absorbing some of the 'scanga' beat.

Martin. Big brother. He was in the army. Training to kill people.

A short walk through the back alley and across the green wheat fields.

They'd not had a chance to ripen yet, but someone had tried to start a fire in the middle of the field. Probably just the little kids playing 'fire engines'. We'd all done it. Set the wheat stubble on fire, call the brigade and help them put it out. It was a laugh. Burnt wheat stubble. Sickly sweet.

*

I headed for the small copse in the corner of two fields. There were a couple of tall beech trees and an ash. A good place to shoot pigeons. I sat down, flattening some golly-wackers to one side, but leaving enough for cover. Wood pigeons were wily bastards. One glimpse of something new and off they'd peel, like fighter jets, and head for the taller trees of the Old Park.

I loaded a single .22 pellet into the barrel of my Webley and waited. I wouldn't cock the gun until the pigeons were spotted, flying in across the fields from where they'd been stuffing their crops. Sitting with it loaded for hours would weaken the spring.

The wait began.

Unlike the rest of Sunday, I could take this shutdown. The slowing, the nothing. I liked the wide focus. The trees had a time scale of their own. The farmed fields rushed and rolled away, but the trees stayed, swayed. Leaves chattering gently in the soft sou-wester. The sea couldn't spit this far, so the air was dry and prickly. Mud crust. Corn stalk. Barbed wire. The thin clouds stretched motionless as they sped by, high above. The trees gripped hard with their roots and stopped us spinning off into the vapour.

Who was I kidding? I couldn't escape it. The sea was pulling the strings even here. It was never distant, no matter how far inland you hid. The clouds were tendrils evaporating from its wet flanks, arching over, bringing moisture to the fire and ash that we sat on. Poor, thirsty wretches, with our body bags sloshing. How long would we last without its moisture? The trees cradled me, their filtering leaves keeping me from perspiring, melting, boiling away into the sun. Its roots, sucking like a baby on the wet soil below. Its trunk and branches masking the tide, rising through the sap.

Come on pigeons.

The trees even bowed to the moon, to the tides, to the fucking sea. All the weeds, the sweet smelling cow parsley on which I sat, waiting. The cabbage white dancing, disabled, from flower head to head. All dried up and blown away without the sea. And all the time it moved, patiently, not with the power and frustration of the storm, but quietly, stealthily, wearing away at the cliff face, the sand dune, the sea wall, eroding layer by layer, particle by particle, taking back what had escaped her.

It must be a 'her'. The land was a 'him'. Showy, arrogant, rocky, hard, stubborn. But all worn away by the greatest force of all, the soft liquid of the sea and the gritty currents that stirred in the black belly of her oceans.

Pigeons. Three.

At last!

They made a wary fly-past. I pulled slowly on cool steel until the spring clicked somewhere inside. The barrel flipped back limply and closed perfectly over the breech. I kept the gun tight against me, motionless, as the clapping wing beats announced their arrival in the branches above.

Wait. Breathe slowly. Calmly. They can even hear your heartbeat.

Your blood pumping.

Wet.

One long minute and they'd settled enough for me to move. Kneeling position. Gun raised slowly, using the trunk as cover. Safety off.

Aim.

Only a head shot was good enough.

Breath.

Moisture.

Squeeze.

The sea.

An explosion of blood sent them in all directions. Feathers busting through leaves and twigs, they peeled away and only reformed the flock when they were high above the fields.

Away.

They were good. They were survivors. A movement in the cow parsley, a scrape of my jacket against the stock of the gun. The hissing sap alerting them to the sore thumb, the sea creature slurping below, out of place.

Me.

I hated them. Their senses perfectly attuned with their world. A world with which I was no longer in step. The beat was now a distant calling rhythm. One I could only listen to from outside the youth club, drunk on cheap cider.

Fuck, I wanted to shoot something.

But I had a code - never kill unless you eat.

A sparrow landed on a branch at the edge of the copse. Twenty feet away. I took aim, carelessly this time hoping to scare it. It sat 'cheeping', uncaring or unwary. A house sparrow. Man-made. Accustomed. Worth less than a pigeon. Worth nothing at all. But still not on my 'fair game' list.

The trigger gave behind my finger and the pellet smacked into the bird, dropping it in a cloud of small feathers. I rushed to the spot, and found it in the nettles. Beak open, tongue beating rhythmically.

A small drop of blood rolled across, beneath its closing eye. It was warm. Soft. Its head lolled over the edge of my fingers. Its nape, conker brown. Wing bars, corn golden.

Dead.

But still perfect.

I scraped a little hole in the field with my fingers and buried it.

To hide my shame.

*

The alley back to the estate was overgrown with weeds and stingers. Hot, green, and littered with broken bikes, smashed TVs and cans; the trees bending over the back gardens of the private houses behind the flint walls were manicured, lopped on one side, and burnt, broken and adorned with bald tyres and glue bags on the other.

My side.

Excited voices inside an elderberry bush ahead alerted me. Johnny Oldman emerged, cupping something in one hand. A BSA Meteor in the other. Two of the Houghton kids were pushing and shoving to get a look at the kill. They saw me coming and Johnny stopped in the middle of the path, smiling. He looked like a ferret. Hateful little dark eyes. A nasty biter. Bobbing. Weaving.

"Alright Jimmy."

The youngsters called me Jimmy. Respect.

I was bigger than them.

"Jimbo, betcha can't hit one of these." Oldman thinks he can take me. A scrap is long overdue. I should have smacked him when we were playing British Bulldog on the Green. When he flattened my pissy brother.

I never forget.

His hand opens and inside a dead blue tit. Green, yellow and natural blue. The smallest pointed beak and shut eyes.

Fucking prick.

He sees I'm not happy. He glimpses my pain. I shut it down and slap the bird from his hand.

"Take it home for your dinner, you've got fuck all else."

I'm a tramp, but he's a beggar.

I can hear his manky teeth grinding as I walk away. His sweat popping. His gun reloading. I turn round and point mine at his eye before he can fit the pellet.

He freezes. He's not sure if I will. Then backs down. A moment of anger fizzles and his shoulders drop. His eyes roll over like puppies. Mine growl like a bitch-fucker. I should smack him. That's the law of our jungle.

But I can't do it. And why? Because as much as I hate it, I'm just like him now.

No. Worse.

We both kill things. He takes pleasure in his ignorance. But I know that everything I destroy kills another part of myself.

The quicker I get this job done the better.

Skanga (Feeling Irie)

Beanie is still at the window of his bedroom playing his boot-boy vinyl. I think he's smoking something. He sees me.

"Tell Martin. Yeah?"

I will. Everything is passed on here. Every comment, message. Every slight. Everything.

Martin. My big brother. Once a skinny little shit with gappy teeth. I don't even know what he looks like now. Different. Not seen him for over a year. Apart from a picture sent from Gibraltar. I loved it. He was stripped to the waist, next to some mad-looking bloke with a droopy black tash. Both threatening us with whips, snarling, pissed. Better than the last photo at school. Mop of hair. Freckles. Stubby teeth.

Martin left the Church of Little England School, and worked in a supermarket. It was that or down the pit. Or the other great employer for us - the Army. He went in, got the beret and now was jumping out of airplanes with a different hat. Everyone else who wasn't in 'The Regiment' was a 'crap hat'.

Don't think the whip was standard issue.

I'd heard my dad boasting once. He'd been in the same mob before he got chucked out.

Front door. Tried to go straight upstairs. I could hear Mum and Dad exchanging. Not quick enough. That bad air again, like when the police had been round. That guilty air when they stood up for me, but knew I'd done it.

Lately, I'd always done it.

I swung open the front room door. Even the dog was sitting up. Mum seemed animated. Upbeat. "Martin's coming home on leave. Tomorrow."

My dad nodded behind his book. "You'll have to give up your bed for him and sleep in with the others."

Great. Piss on me.

"I've put fresh sheets on."

Like that's going to make everything cosy.

Mum lit a menthol cigarette and twirled the smoke towards the back of the sofa.

"Get anything?"

I slipped the gun off my shoulder and shook my head. Too ashamed to look at her. "Don't worry. There's some roast in the oven."

Sunday roast, of course.

Upstairs I laid the gun on the bed and opened the record player. Overplayed, brother-scratched vinyl slid from a yellow sleeve. The heavy plastic arm lifted and stopped abruptly over the spinning disc. The crackle of the needle in the groove sent shivers.

The Pistols. A little bit of anarchy.

Sunday couldn't be shattered, but at least the noise helped. Monday was coming and now I'd left school, it was gonna get even worse. I was gonna be sixteen soon. I was gonna have to get a job.

Could join the Army?

Yeah. Stick a heated bayonet up my arse.

I'd just have to do what everyone else did round here.

Go on the rock'n'roll.

Like Clockwork

My birthday passed, just like the one before, only slower. I got a few cards and a fiver. Hooray. I was sixteen. I could legally have sex.

My dad bought me a new watch. Don't know why. I don't like watches. Time to me seems to run in all directions, like liquid metal. Not little tick-tocks of the ever-marching clock. Forward. Click. Forward. Clack. Like some machine.

Time was definitely liquid.

Fucking sea again.

Incoming.

Pushing me.

We were meeting Martin at the train station. But first I had to sign on.

The first time I'd been to the dole office was with my dad. I used to go there when my mum wasn't around to look after me. She'd be working on the potato fields. Spud picking.

I can remember the dole was a big, grey stone building, which we got to through a dank alley. There were windows with bars on the outside. My dad would get all sing-songy when he got to that alley.

It seemed like a happy place to me. There were lots of his friends gathered there. The jokes would pass back and forth as we'd stand in line. My dad would get to the counter and let go of my hand. I'd look around. With the eyes of a four year old, it might as well have been a party. But there were no drinks or food. Lots of smoke. Like my nan's funeral. But nobody crying. But the same softly spoken voices, exchanging private business at the counter.

I could never understand why they were always arguing at home about this dole thing. Sometimes my dad went out, came home covered in mud and smelling of dust. Concrete. He'd give Mum 'housekeeping'. Sometimes he'd go out and come back drunk. There'd be a big fight. Lots of quiet time for him, sitting in his chair, reading. Then came the mysterious time 'on the dole'.

Now it was my turn.

I handed the woman my I.D. Behind me, banter. Buzz. Ahead, a deadened muffle of paper. A form and some questions, and a signature. I got my signing-on card and joined the club.

No big deal. I don't know what all the fuss was about. They all seemed pretty friendly. Like the people who worked at the bank or at the police station. Helpful, now the shit was theirs to deal out.

*

The train station was twenty minutes walk. My new watch said so. The town looked the same as ever. Victorian. Urchins 'n' all. The station used to be on the beach, when the town was popular. When people used to come to bathe in its medicinal waters. Now it was about a mile and a half away, high and dry at the top end of town and the sea was mainly used to water down sewage.

Mum met me at the station entrance. She waved excitedly. "C'mon, Martin's train's just got in."

We jogged down the echoing stairs into the platform underpass. The train chuntered in. Doors opened and slammed shut. My dad stood at the front of our family queue, waiting, my little brothers clutched to his side for their own safety. They'd been allowed to miss the last day of school especially! Sitting on the bench, my sister Debbie was smoking a fag disinterestedly. She'd be the next to go, like my other two half-sisters. They pissed-off as soon as they got jobs. Or a bloke to move in with.

We approached the happy throng. Martin, dressed in his smart uniform and carrying a big rucksack, marched into view. Mum rushed past Dad and flung her arms around him. He shook her off, embarrassed.

"We thought we'd missed you."

Martin looked at his watch and snapped. "On time." His time was proper. Army time. Mechanical. Marching on in step. Tick-fucking-tock.

My dad puffed out his chest.

"Welcome home, son."

Martin ignored his hand and snarled playfully at my little brothers. They jumped him. In a show of strength he picked them both up, on one arm, and spun them around, frightening Mum to death as their legs flailed close to the departing train.

Debbie kissed him on the cheek and said goodbye.

"Got to be at work now." Martin nodded. "And don't eat my chocolate!" A private joke between them. He'd never been officially caught, but she knew it was him that devastated her stash before he went away.

Then Martin stared at me.

I peeped back, dropping my head guiltily. He'd changed. He was taller. Broader. His face harder. His eyes like cold, quarried rock. I didn't like what I saw. He was proud. Asking to be worn away.

A flash of suspicion or something registered in his eyes.

I knew he'd caught a glimpse of the sea, through me.

He sized the enemy up, then jabbed me dismissively on the shoulder. "Let's get this lot home. I'm starving."

For all he cared, the tempest could bash against him forever. He was granite. Atoms bonded tight. Intrusive.

Forged by fire.

What a Waste

Martin dropped his stuff into our room. My bed was really the only option. Nobody went in Debbie's room, not unless they wanted to be choked in their sleep from the hairspray and perfume she'd roll in. They couldn't put Martin in with Pissy Pants and the Nightmare Kid. So, my bed it was. But that was good, meant I could convince Mum to let me sleep on the sofa. I could sneak the TV back on when Dad went to bed.

Taking us by surprise, the first thing Martin did when he got home was to fill a massive punch-bag with sand, 'borrowed' from the building site round the corner. He hung it on a branch of the big, old cherry tree in the back garden, then disappeared into the bedroom for about an hour. I went in while he was having a bath and saw his civvie kit all laid out on my bed. Neat lines and rows of unrolled clothes.

After his bath, he shaved and got dressed up to go out. Now he was in the living room, with us all, stuffing his face. I sat on the arm of the sofa, behind Mum, and watched him wipe out his shepherd's pie she'd made especially.

He was hungry. He ate in fast, precise movements, chewing each mouthful three times before swallowing. No pleasure. Just feeding. Energy boosting.

Pissy and Nightmare had already lost interest and were chasing each other mindlessly, up and down the stairs.

"Where are you going tonight?" Mum asked.

"Dunno."

"I've made your bed up. You can sleep in Jimmy's."

"I know."

Munch munch, chew swallow. He was in the room, but wasn't. He was eating his dinner, but not tasting it. He was refuelling. He caught me watching him and locked on.

"You working yet?"

Crunch, slurp, suck, gulp.

"Nah. Signing on."

"You should join up. You don't wanna be a waster." He tipped the plate and let the last bit of gravy drop onto his tongue. Gauge on full. Definitely not a waster.

"Didn't do me no harm," chirped Dad.

Martin looked at me again, this time smiling cruelly. "Like I said, you don't want to end up a waster."

"Cheeky bugger!" said Dad, elated. Banter. It was their bond. "You're not talking to a crap-hat here, you know!"

Martin rose quickly, taking the plate to the kitchen. He ruffled my old man's long, blond, hippy-hair as he passed.

"You wanna get that cut. You look like Colonel Custer." Insult. My dad thought of himself as an Apache. We all laughed. Big Chief Armchair General.

"That's a beer you owe me!"

Martin dropped the plate in the sink and shouted back. "I'm meeting up with Beanie."

"What time will you be home?" Mum asked feebly.

"Dunno. Might be going to a club."

"You've got your key?"

"Yeah."

Back door opened and slammed shut. Dad looked sulky. Mum lit up and started to unwrap a smoking sweet. "He didn't even say goodbye."

"He's in the army now," said Dad, picking up his open book from the arm of the chair. "Doesn't need our permission."

"But still... do you think he's got a girl to see?'

"He's going to see his mates."

"He's a bit... in a rush?"

"He's only got forty eight hours leave. No time to waste."

"Oh. Yes," puffed Mum. Disappointment hanging on her ciggy-lips. "What do you think he'll want for breakfast?"

Dad ignored her. The book was drawing him in, somewhere safe. Stable. Somewhere foreign. He'd heard but wasn't listening. His irritation would show if he continued to be present. He'd been waiting for Martin to come home and take him out for a pint. To talk shit about the army. Man stuff. But he'd been passed over for a subordinate. Beanie. Now, there was a waster. Mum looked over and offered me a sweet.

"You okay with sleeping on the sofa tonight?"

Of course. No problem. I take a sweet. I'll wash the paper off.

"No he's not."

"Oh stop being grouchy."

"I'm not being anything. He's not sleeping on the sofa."

"Why not? Martin's got his bed. He's sixteen now."

"He'll be up all night watching TV."

"There's nothing on."

"He falls asleep and it stays on all night. Bloody waste of electricity."

"I'll come down."

"You what? You'll be asleep by nine!"

"That's because I get up for you in the morning."

"You don't have to."

"Who's going to get you off to work then?"

Pause. Change of page. Same chapter. Old book.

"I'm not going in tomorrow."

Mum stopped her fag drag half way through her suck. The menthol smoke soured.

He'd done it again.

"You said the job would last for another six weeks!"

"Graham let me down. Got another foreman in, and he had his own gang."

"Bloody brilliant. Now what are we going to do?"

Dad started tapping. The page stopped turning. He was yanked back in.

"Sign on?" I suggested.

"Shut up, you waster."

"Don't take it out on him 'cause you lost your bloody job again!"

That was my cue to exit. Upstairs. Fight my little brothers. Cover them from the row downstairs. They knew. Their eyes were saucer-sad radars.

I hit them with a pillow and wrestled them onto the bed. Pissy started throwing stuffed toys while Nightmare hit me with a heavy bolster. I lay back and let them get the better of me. What else could I do? Singe or Bill wouldn't be out on a Monday. Nobody on the estate was out on a Monday. Wednesday was giro day. Thursday was a pint and a game of Space Invaders to plan for Friday. Saturday as well, if we had the money.

Smack. Pillow too hard in the face. Time to duff them up a bit. My weapon of choice, the snake-shaped draught excluder. Time for a thrashing. Better show them who's boss.

Little fucking wasters.

No More Heroes

The night passed. It always did. Funny that. The world keeps turning, night fades into day, then back comes the night. The moon rises, tides pulled back and forth. Birds fly south only to return in spring and yet, I reckon us humans are trying very hard to stand still. Hoping that life won't notice us. That we can be excused. I've got a note from my mum somewhere that says 'James can't take part in life today, he's hurt his wrist'.

Wanker.

The TV buzzing in the corner roused me. I turned it off at the plug and peeked through the blinds. It was the black and white fuzz of early morning. Through its grainy haze, I saw something that made my day start moving.

In the front garden was a large, white spoiler from the twatty car two doors down. The Gordons. It belonged to the youngest one, Brian. He was working for an estate agent or something poncey like that. Went to work in the morning in a cheap suit from Burtons.

His girlfriend Becky had nice tits though.

It looked like someone had ripped the spoiler clean off his Cortina and planted it in our garden. It wasn't hard to work out who. He was lying asleep, not far from it, in the hedge.

I opened the front door. Quietly. It was early. Too fucking early for me and, luckily, too early for anyone else to be out, off to work. Especially Brian Gordon. He worked nine to five. He would still be in bed, wanking himself off, thinking about his girlfriend's tits.

I would be. Even with that note from my mum.

"Martin." I whispered. But he was out cold. Still pissed up. "Wake up you prat."

I picked up the spoiler and poked him in the gut with it.

"Martin. Wake up."

Martin really woke up.

He ripped the spoiler from my hands and threw it over the hedge into the road, all in one movement. Then stood there, fists clenched, ready to fight his attacker.

"It's me. Jimmy."

"Thought it was the crocodile," was all he said before walking inside, slamming the door behind him. Leaving me standing barefoot in the garden, in a pair of y-fronts.

Good job I'd broken in through the bathroom window so many times that it hardly bothered to resist. A few quiet taps and the latch would pop, allowing me to reach in and open the main window.

I lay back down on the sofa, waiting for one of the only nine-to-fivers in the street to get off to work and the shit to hit the fan.

Martin was nestling down in my bed after a night in the hedge-hammock. I could hear him snoring above me. I switched on the TV and slid the volume down. I watched the dots of the shutdown swarming across the screen like confused bees and drifted into a doze. Trying all the time, not to think about Becky's cleavage. Those tight, cap-sleeved t-shirts pulling her breasts into the shape of warm, oven-baked puddings...

Mum nearly caught me knocking one out. She seemed more excited about something other than me. She went to the blinds. "Look. Quick. It's Brian's car." I pretended to be a little interested and joined her. Dragging the blankets with me.

She tilted the pink and yellow metal slats, so we could just about peer between them. "Someone smashed it last night."

Really?

Brian stood by the Cortina. The broken spoiler was laid on the roof. In his hand he held the massive CB aerial, explaining to his mum where it had once been joined to the car.

Martin walked through the room scratching his bollocks and disappeared into the toilet.

"Do you think Martin might have seen something, last night?"

"Dunno. I was asleep when he came in."

Martin exited the toilet, still scratching his crotch.

Crabs, I bet.

"What's up?"

"Someone smashed-up Brian Gordon's car last night."

Martin opened the blind up wide and looked out.

"Pillock."

Mum quickly slapped it shut, to hide her nosing. Martin smiled at me behind her back and jogged upstairs.

"Do you think, Martin..." Mum looked at me, excitedly. Could he? Would he? "No. I don't think he would...." Then she giggled, naughtily. "I suppose that's what you get for having a flash car like that up here."

Martin came back down, dressed in tracksuit, trainers and a t-shirt.

"Going for a run."

"Don't you want any breakfast?" Mum said, hoping she'd be useful.

"Later."

He skipped out of the front door, vaulted the chain-linked fence and jogged past Brian Gordon and his mum, offering them a hearty "Good morning." They spluttered a few words as he accelerated out of the estate towards the park and the sea.

I turned away to hide my smirking face. Mum prattled on about Mrs. Gordon, and how this would bring forward her first drink of the day. I left her to her bitching, pulled on my jeans and went into the back garden. The punchbag was hanging there. I gave it a light, celebratory smack. Shit! It was Solid.

Sand to polish his stone hands.

Inside I heard Mum shouting the kids down for breakfast. Summer holidays had begun. If I hung around, she'd have me babysitting. I opted to raid the cornflakes before my little brothers came to fight over the biggest bowl. The red plastic one. Always the best thing about sleeping on the sofa. Get to the bowl first.

I sat on the back step, with a brew and munched the cornflakes while my brothers whined about the small white bowls filled by Mum. Dry flakes for

Nightmare and with extra sugar for Pissy.

Nightmare started rooting around in the cupboard under the sink. He pulled out a large casserole dish and started to fill it with more flakes. Mum took it away. He started freaking out as usual until she gave in. This set Pissy off, complaining. I threw him the empty red bowl and he did a victory lap of the tiny kitchen holding it aloft like the world cup.

"I got the red bowl. I got the red bowl."

Nightmare slapped the bowl from his older brother and it span. The breakfast fight began. Mum dragged them apart and threatened Pissy with no beach, no trip to the fun fair, no pictures, no nothing, ever.

Nightmare got the red bowl and sat on the sofa eating cornflakes, one at a time with his fingers, while Mum started digging in the pile of clothes in the cupboard under the stairs. Looking for rags.

She needed money.

Every Saturday morning, when we nagged her to go to the pictures, she'd get in that cupboard and drag out the rags. Stuffed into carrier bags, she'd load them into the big old pram for us to take down to Newbury's. The rag-and-bone yard. Wool always fetched the most.

There seemed to be an unending supply beneath the stairs. Mostly hand-me-downs from Auntie Joy. Stuff from friends. Rags to start with. But we'd get to try them on for Mum and she'd do her best to convince us they looked okay. Hideous patterned shirts, crimpolene flares, with a few iron-shaped burn marks on. Not fit for Auntie Joy's posh kids to wear, but good enough for scummers like us.

She wasn't even our auntie. Just someone Mum had done some cleaning for once. She used to pop in and see Mum, but would spend hours arguing politics with Dad. Until he'd go too far and get personal. It was always the same. She'd storm off in a huff and Mum would nag Dad for being rude. He could never lose an argument with Auntie Joy, or with anyone, for that matter.

The back gate slammed open and Martin crouched, breathing deeply. Sweaty. Dripping. Muscles tight. Veins inflated.

"Where did you run to?"

"Dargate."

Fucking hell. That was five miles away. Without warning he stood up straight, marched to the punch bag and began.

Smack, smack, kick, smack smack smack. A flurry of combinations. Grunting, puffing, but working from beyond breath or sweat. Pure guts.

After ten minutes he stopped, face red, eyes engorged. Fists clenched, knuckles bleeding. Then he started his press-ups. On four fingers, then two, followed by ones just on his knuckles.

Shit, he was like Bruce Lee!

Then back to the punch bag for a final assault. This included knees and head-butts.

He wasn't like Bruce Lee. Bruce Lee was human!

The punch bag swung silently beneath the creaking cherry tree. A few leaves fell down around him. Martin grabbed my cup of tea and sat down next to me, on the step, catching his breath.

"Training," was all he said.

I didn't know how to answer. I'd never seen anyone move that much, with such purpose. Such violence. He saw that I was stunned and laughed.

"Fancy a pint tonight?"

"On a Tuesday?"

Martin seemed puzzled. Every day was a drinking day for him.

"I ain't got no money. Don't get my giro 'till tomorrow."

"No problem. I'm buying. I owe ya one. For not telling Mum."

I nodded. Glad to have been of service.

Martin went in for a bath. I stood before the punch bag, wondering. In another life, another time, could I have joined the Army?

The careers advisor at school thought so.

I was taken from my class, without warning and marched into the library. An overweight man in an ill-fitting suit sat before me. I was immediately distracted by the fact that I could see his hairy belly between his shirt buttons. I tried not to stare. He looked very briefly at my 'file'.

"What do you want to do with yourself?"

I didn't understand the question.

"What interests you?"

Girls. Football. Fossils. Birds. Then I remembered I was at school. He was at school. He must be talking about something school related.

"Environmental science." I answered swiftly. "It's my favourite subject."

He glanced at the file again, then back at me without a pause and said, "Ever thought about joining the Army?"

Sure, I like shooting things and loved tanks, used to draw them all the time. Spent half my kiddy life playing 'war' on the Green outside the house. Or my favourite - 'best man's fall'. It worked like this - one volunteers to be the shooter, while the others line up and take it in turn to be killed. You'd call out the weapon of your execution and try to die in the best possible way to win. I single-handedly created the hand-grenade forward somersault, which always won as no one else could flip over, legs and arms flailing and land without breaking something.

On other, rainy Sundays, I'd line up soldiers indoors, behind the sofa and fight my little brother's armies. The rules of engagement - one shot for a rifle to kill one enemy soldier. Machine guns could take out three. Grenade - as many as my finger could knock over before Pissy would start squealing enough to annoy those watching telly.

Believe me, I never had a problem with the Army, or war. That was until my dad let me stay up to watch a programme, one wet Wednesday.

The World At War. On ITV.

I was twelve.

I became an avid watcher. Each week I'd sit with my dad, little brothers in bed, and Mum asleep on the sofa. It was our treat. Something Dad could talk at me about. He knew every general and every battle.

I became entranced by the black and white footage of disheveled men, shuffling in unending lines, clothed in rags, spirits broken, eyes filled with suffering, regret and pain. Corpses being bulldozed into pits. Victims of the concentration camps, staring out from behind barbed wire, past caring. No tanks or soldiers charging for their cause, their comrades. No flags waving, no victories, no heroes. Just silence and despair.

In this version of war, nobody seemed to win anything.

Not even the high ground.

The driest of dry land.

Risen up from the sea.

I looked at the careers advisor and laughed.

He sighed deeply and shut my file. I thought the button on his shirt was going to pop and take my eye out.

And that was that.

Me? Join the Army? Die in horrible ways or have your spirit broken, crushed within you? I couldn't find that in the brochure. Sure, I'd fight the Nazis if they invaded. Have to. But go and fight someone else's war? Fuck that. You'd have to be some sort of mental.

I looked at the punch bag hanging, a dead weight amputee beneath the graceful cherry tree.

I was going out with him tonight.

To drink.

On a Tuesday.

That was really mental.

Five Minutes

The Royal was the largest pub on the seafront. It was the place to go for a fight. Even if your weren't looking for one, there was always someone looking for you. Screwing you out.

Inside it was large, basic. One long bar, a few tables and a small black dance floor. Up a tight flight of stairs was a saloon bar which hid the pool table. The pool cues were kept behind the bar for their own safety. Until recently, we'd always been thrown out before we could buy our first drink. They didn't want us 'under-agers'. People who'd glass you, or snap a pool cue over your head, were okay with the management, who happened to be the biggest load of cunts in Broadgate.

They called themselves Rent-a-Riot. Small time villains and petty thieves from the other side of town. From a bigger estate than ours. Seddington. Rent-a-Riot were made up from two of Seddington's finest families, mingled by inbreeding. On their own, they were fat, badly tattooed men in their thirties. But together, they sorted things out. They were big men in a small town.

Since my stunt with the fire extinguisher, Bill didn't think we should go anywhere near the place. Oily Harry was in the middle of the gang, not the leader, but big enough to ignite the others.

If he recognised me it was shit creek. Paddle inserted.

We stood glued, outside the entrance to the saloon, until curiosity got the better of us. Singe popped his head inside. The bar was empty and unmanned. Clear. He called us in.

Looking down into the main bar, there was a fat girl at the till. Not the guy who chased us out with a baseball bat. Stage One complete.

Stage Two - find brother.

The etched glass of a dividing wall obscured the view into the main bar. But it looked busy, for a Tuesday. Two groups of men drank and laughed in an exaggerated way, finding everything they said extra funny. The jukebox played some disco shit. They all seemed to be into disco shit. Probably thought they could pull birds when they were dancing. A couple of Bacardi and cokes would pull any of the slags who drank in the Royal. Ankle tattoos. Fuck-me-arse stilettos. Hooped earrings. Smoke-cracked, hag-cackle voices. Tight, short dresses from the market. Second kid bellies.

Class.

Most of them liked starting fights.

Some of them did the fighting.

We snuck down into the main bar. Nobody paid more than a glance.

Relief. No Oily Harry.

Martin stood behind them, on the other side. Alone. Drinking like he ate. Lift, tip, glug, replace on bar. Again. Lift, tip, glug...

One of the Royalettes was eyeing him up. She approached as we did.

"Got a light mate?"

It was always the first question.

"Don't smoke."

She turned and cackled to her friend. Fatter. Brown, spud-picking hands. Chewed fingernails.

"He don't smoke."

"Wonder what else he don't do." They both laughed. Martin ignored them. Ordered another pint. Smoker leaned on the bar next to him. Her titty-tatts bulging.

"'Ere luv. My friend thinks you're a poof!"

Martin paid for his drink and spoke without looking at her. "If you can bend over and touch your toes fatty, I'll fuck both of you from behind."

Foreplay.

Nice.

"You gonna buy me a drink first." Martin turned his head slowly, deliberately, and looked her in the eye.

"You gonna suck my cock first?"

She's insulted. Drinks always come before blow jobs.

Martin carried on with his pint. Smoker clattered off to her friend. Face like thunder.

I think this maybe a good moment to make contact.

Martin looked past me at Bill and Singe. "I said I'd buy you a pint, not your mates."

Bill pulled a fiver from his pocket and bought himself and Singe a drink. He offered Martin one. Martin grinned, Cheshire style.

"Whiskey. Cheers."

I could see him writing 'crap hat' all over them.

Bill and Singe shuffled. Uncomfortably.

Eyes across the bar are suddenly on us.

The Smoker is talking to one of the Rent-a-Riot mob. A thick-necked, cave-dweller called Staples. Kev and his elder brother Billy ran the crew. They've noticed Martin. An outsider. Someone who insults 'birds'.

That's their job.

Bill and Singe retreat to a table in an alcove across the bar, away from their gaze, leaving me and Martin to talk.

"They're alright." I try to convince. "My best mates."

"Never seen them up the street before."

Martin's eyes are looking at me, but he can sense something. A bristling of animal instincts are focused in the back of his eye. A pinpoint of intensity.

"They don't live up Prestwell. But they're alright. Singe is a right laugh." Martin suddenly gives me fifty pence.

"Go and put something better on the juke box."

I wander over. It's near to where Bill and Singe are sitting. They sense it too. A build up of man static. A testosterone charge, arcing.

Bill wants to go.

Kev Staples is standing too close to Martin at the bar.

We know what happens next.

The rest of the gang, about four of them, loiter, trying to look distant. Uninvolved.

But their fists are tightening.

They laugh falsely and whisper, nervously to the slags. The static is building to a current and flows between them. Crawling across the velour walls, it makes the hair on my neck spike.

Singe also wants to go now.

I want to watch. I've seen him 'training'. My money's already down.

Sparks spit from Kev's mouth. Something about the slag, his 'girlfriend'. Apologies insisted. Casual pretext.

I'm watching, in slow motion.

Martin turns his back, ignoring Staples.

One rough finger pokes his immovable granite shoulder.

Strike.

Martin grabs. Snaps the finger back and butts Staples on the nose.

Crack.

The tension ignites.

Lunge. Grapple. Smash.

Beer and glass wasted over the bar.

The four watching are sprung. Punches. Kicks. Bottles. A bar stool helps Martin on his way down. Fists and feet engulf him, like a stampede. Kev and Billy leading the charge.

Bill tries to drag me out. But I can't move.

Paralysed by violence, I stand transfixed.

A slag hits Martin with a bottle. It doesn't break on his muscled back.

That's all I can see of him. His arched back as he curls into a tight ball on the floor.

Still they kick. But slower now. The blows becoming less frequent.

They're puffing through gritted teeth. Fat bellies. Lifestyles weighing them down.

Bill has seen enough and runs.

Singe wants to, but like me, his boots are riveted to the floor.

The last blows are Kev's. He tries to turn Martin with his foot, so he can punch his face. Break his nose.

A roar from the floor snaps me back into real time.

Kev flies through the air, onto his arse, as Martin rises.

The other attackers back away. Bewildered.

Martin rips his shirt from his own back and throws it. Laughing. His chiseled body is wet with beer, sweat and blood.

But he is just... laughing.

"C'mon then!" Is all he says, almost playfully, as he knocks one of them to the floor with a single, straight punch.

The older, harder brother, Billy.

Two run as their big man goes down. Kev hesitates. His brother is spark out and his mates gone. He tries for the door, but Martin steps in in his way.

Smiling.

Time for the kill.

Martin bombards him with fast combos.

He becomes the swinging punch bag.

Staples buries his head to escape the blows. He's bigger and weighs more, and manages to pull Martin down to the floor.

Now he realises his mistake.

Epileptic, he tries to escape Martin's snake-like constriction, his every muscle heaving, spasmodic.

Martin puts his head in a death lock. His fist battering his face, again and again.

Wave after wave.

Staples blocks with hopeless, desperate fingers.

Martin tears them away and clamps his free hand down on Staples' forehead.

Two fingers gouge, deeply into screwed-up eye sockets.

Staples screams and thrashes. Blood running down his cheeks.

"MARTIN!"

My shout is desperate enough to halt him.

His programmed eyes locate me.

They are alive.

Animal.

No.

Human.

Conscious. Choosing. Hurting.

Martin sees the horror reflected and stops.

Staples stumbles to his feet, half-blind, blinking, trying to work out where he is. Why he is.

Martin pushes him contemptuously into a chair with the flat of his foot.

Heart rates flatline. A begrudging silence falls.

The slags attend Staples with bar towels. Whispering. Hoping not to attract the attention of the man-beast.

He grabs a glass and finishes a pint.

His pint. The only one left standing.

He wipes the blood from his face with his ripped shirt and grins at me and Singe. "Wanna go somewhere else?"

It's always spectacular. When liquid meets rock.

Toiler On The Sea

I borrowed a bike the next day. Mine was knackered. I promised myself I'd put it back where I 'found it' later.

I cycled as far as I could from Broadgate, out past the power station, over the river to The Bay. It was quiet there. My secret place. I used to come here with a teacher from school, the only one that I liked. He was part of the Bird Observatory and could name every bird, mammal and plant and explain how they were all knitted together. Dependent. It made sense. This natural world made perfect sense.

I laid the bike down in the marram grass in the dunes. The rest of the way to The Point was on foot. There were nesting birds. The bike might disturb them.

I liked to sit and watch the terns fishing, feeding their young. Time swirled in a slow eddy here and I lost hours. But here also, I found myself a place that reflected what I felt inside.

It was a hard place, but not forced, erected in months like Prestwell. Its solid foundation laid over thousands of years by the light hand of the wind and rain. Sculpted, chip by chip. Stone by stone. Grain by grain. A masterpiece created by the sea. A difficult place to remain for the birds, insects, plants and mammals that strived here. But a perfect place to be alive, if even for a brief moment.

I sat and breathed the light sea air. Trying to reconnect.

Across the Bay, the white cliffs of Broadgate looked small. The town a model. Here, I was a giant. The elements lifting me, stretching me, thinning me until I almost didn't exist. My ego fluttered like a small paper kite carried on some eternal, unseen breeze.

For a moment I became part of it again.

Just one moment.

Then, self consciously, I looked down and saw myself hiding in the dunes. Conspicuous.

Detached.

Out of place.

What I once possessed, through a longing, instinctive awareness, had gone.

Forever?

I was a human animal, evolved to cope with a different jungle now. I'd grow hard like the brick walls and concrete of the estate. Man-made.

A towering folly. Strong externally, but inherently weak.

Dysfunctional. Estranged from my natural mother, I had filled up with frustration. A hatred grown of what I'd become. Separate. Individual.

Alone.

I tossed a flint pebble into the brackish pond behind, scaring a dragonfly to flight. What a wasted journey. I could no longer stay here, anymore than the waves could turn from the shore, from the pebbles they ground.

Perfectly. Rounded.

Broadgate was my environment now. I had to stop fighting it. Stop hating it. I belonged to Prestwell. I knew it had more work to do, before it finished misshaping me. Creating my hopeless defense against the sea.

Burning Up Time

Singe wanted to meet. He was still buzzing about the fight in The Royal. Bill had been giving him gyp and needed sorting out. Everyone up the street had heard about the fight. Everyone in Broadgate. I'd grow a couple of milk crates taller off the back of it. But Bill was bitching. It was time for another whinge session. But at least there was a pint in it for me. Singe had got a tax rebate and it was Friday.

Lunchtime.

We met in The Rising Sun. It was only just past opening time, so it made talking a bit.... whispery.

We set up the pool table. It was out of earshot of the landlord.

Bill weighed in first.

"What was all that about, with your brother?" I broke the pack with a sharp crack. Balls rolled. None tumbled. I was never lucky at breaking. Singe took the cue from me and lined up a shot.

I shrugged my shoulders at Bill. What was he on about?

"Rent-a-riot! We could have been done, bad."

"Are they looking for us?" said Singe.

Tension as the ball dropped and rolled. Bill's family knew one of them. Half-related. He'd know if.

"Nah. But that's not the point."

Singe lined up another shot.

"Staples won't be looking for us anyway. He's got no eyes!" I laughed.

Bill shook his head. "This ain't a joke. Your brother's a maniac."

"So?"

Singe skewed the cue deliberately, sending the ball flying from the table. It hit the wall and bounced onto the hard floor. Bill stopped it with his foot and picked it up.

"So," he said, threatening me with the chipped white cue ball, "if you think we're hanging about with your brother, you're madder than I thought."

They didn't get it. Martin just kicked the crap out of some of the cuntiest people in Broadgate, making it a safer place for us in the process.

I said something like that to Bill. Then we got to the nub. The point.

"It's always just the three of us. I just don't trust him." Bill was possessive. Being the 'hard one' of the group was his job. He wasn't much of a fighter, but he was big for his age and strong. Broad. A couple of fights in school and people had heard of him. They let him be. Martin was stepping on his toes.

I gave Bill the pool cue. I had an easy shot on the red. "Take it."

Bill slid the cue between his stumpy fingers and took aim. I gave Singe the sly. He smacked the cue at just the right time, making it plough across the table. Spilling balls all over.

He got angry. Bear angry. "You fucking prick. Whaddya do that for!" He tried to smack me with the pool cue. A little slap, but enough to hurt, if I hadn't taken it on the sleeve of my leather.

Singe threw the chalk at him, cracking him on the forehead. "Who's the maniac now?" Bill went pop, chasing us round the pool table, wielding the heavy end of the stick. He smacked Singe on the back of the leg, bringing him down. The cue was pulled back and ready to smack me. I picked up a ball and launched it at him. It missed and smashed a clean hole in the window.

The landlord shouted and shuffled. The bar flap lifted and banged. I acted quickly, knocking an empty onto the floor. Singe stood in front of the hole.

"Sorry Sid," I said sweetly, "knocked it with the pool cue. Accident."

He scowled, but couldn't be bothered. "I'll get the dustpan."

Singe started pulling faces as he cleaned it up. He almost caught us. But we stayed straight. Got away with it. Again. He shuffled back behind the bar. "And no piano today."

Warning taken.

For now.

"Where we going tonight?" Bill said, landing three fresh pints onto the table.

"The Royal." I said, and got kicked for my effort.

"Lords?" Singe muted. We hadn't been there for a while. It was a disco on the sea front, not far from the fight pub.

"Nah. Shitty disco." I didn't fancy it.

"There doing a punk night." Bill seemed keen. "That DJ said."

"Bollocks. Disco-dancing Dick! Who told you that?"

"Leach."

"Leachy speed freak!" spat Singe. "He talks mucho-bollocko!"

Bill was adamant. "They're definitely having a punk night once a month. With a band."

I needed convincing. "What band?"

"Some locals."

"Who?"

"Leach said that Flea and Mark Headon had put a band together and were playing at Lords." We laughed together. It was going to be crap. But we were going. But first, fuel. Drink up. No alcohol allowed in the club. "Just hope his brother's not going to be there." I heard the tail end as I went to piss. Bill worried too much. Martin's kung-fu fighting had given us a 'get out of jail free' card.

"Sorry about the glass." I said cheekily. The landlord thought about it, then waved us and it away. His regulars would be in soon. All two of them. They would sit and put the world to rights while we did our best to smash it into manageable little pieces.

Bodies

A short walk and we were at Bill's house. It was a box with four floors. But in a posh street. Bill's room was right at the top. A palace compared to my gaff. He had his own room for a start. On the wall was a mural painted by his cousin - a horned devil with a naked girl draped over him. Tits all shot out in target practice. In the corner next to his bed was his pride and joy, his home-made stereo. Bill was very handy with electrics.

I opened the airing cupboard, while Singe dragged Bill's air rifle out from under the bed.

"Oi! Wait up." Bill pulled me away from the cupboard. He wanted to reveal the prize himself - a demijohn filled with pints and pints of amber shite. His brother Fagg, named it "Wilfsberg". Fagg lived downstairs and spent his time when he wasn't at Uni, combing his long hair and staging Rush songs in front of his mirror. He called Bill "Wilf" after some comic book character 'Wear 'em out Wilf'. Bill was clumsy alright, but nobody called him Wilf unless they wanted a slap. But the brew got stuck with the name, because we couldn't think of a better one.

Bill decanted some Wilfsberg into a large glass jug and stuck it into his new fridge.

"Where'd that fridge come from?" said Singe, taking out the devil's eye with a crack shot.

"Back of a lorry. Mum said Uncle Stan brought two and couldn't fit both into his garage, or some shit like that. He probably stole the fucking lot."

Bill didn't like his mum's connections. Rent-a-Riot included.

"It does the job though." He said with a cheesy grin. Another jug filled earlier, came out. Frosted over. Ice cold. That was the only way to drink Wilfsberg. It was so putrid. The colder it was, the less slime it left on your pallet. You still had to drink it whilst pinching your bloody nose.

Bill filled three glasses and we chugged the horrible liquid down in one. "One down. Three to go." Bill always said that when we got Wilfed-up. Four pints was all you needed. It was bitter and disgusting, but at least it was strong.

Bill fired up the stereo. As ever, it was Pink Fucking Floyd.

'Wish You Were Here.'

"Wish it was beer." Singe sang.

"Instead of piss." I added.

Bill was getting right into it, ignoring us and singing away. "We're just two lost souls, swimming in a fish bowl... year after year..." I didn't mind, it was his gaff after all. Just wish he'd stop tapping me and pointing out bits of the lyrics he thought I'd like or find intelligent.

More Wilfsberg. Potshots out of the window at the street light, while he was having a piss. 'Dark Side of the Moon' was next. We didn't care by then. Pint three. We had to slow down. It was over two hours before the club opened its doors.

Lull.

Singe made his excuses suddenly and went home.

Me and Bill. Just the two of us. It always got deep. Not ocean deep. Just Bill deep. Like a low pressure descending.

"I know why you see things, MJ." He called me MJ. Mad Jim. Everyone in the 'gang' should have a nickname.

"When you're tripping. Well, you don't actually see things. I think you're just releasing stuff from your brain."

"I don't see stuff when I'm tripping. I am stuff when I'm tripping. I don't have a brain. It's shot-ta-shit."

"Nah. I mean all that stuff about the sea."

"I wasn't tripping. I was shagging."

"Yeah, but you've seen stuff when you're tripping. Glue sniffing. You told us."

I bit my lip.

More Wilfsberg needed.

The stuff in the fridge wasn't cold enough yet.

"Let's wait 'till Singe gets back."

Bill replaced the jug and shut the fridge door.

"Where's he gone?"

"I think he's going to parley with his old man. Try and straighten things out."

"About what?"

"He wants him to go in the Army."

I laughed. Wasn't going to happen. Not in a million years.

"His dad's a twat."

"Yeah, but he could get a trade in there."

"Like my brother?"

"He's gotta do something. You should do something."

Here we go. Scratched record time.

"You're intelligent. I know you try to hide it, but you are." Another one of his blinding insights.

"I did see something once. When I was on mushrooms."

"What?"

Easily distracted.

"Singe laying on a bed of pennies."

Intrigued.

"Pennies?"

"Yeah. Just lying there. On his back. Like he was sleeping. Smiling."

Bill chuckled. His friendly laugh.

"That's what I was saying. Those things you see are projections of stuff flying about in your cranky head. The drugs just let them out."

I was lying. I hadn't seen it on mushrooms. It was a dream. Definitely stuff flying about in my cranky head. But it was a premonition. It had a different feel to it. It wasn't dream textured. Not silk, flowing in the wind, with the dolly mixtures of my mind tumbling after it.

It was air. It was the breeze. A sea breeze. It was atmospheric. I was breathing it. Not dreaming it. That's how I knew it was real. But I couldn't explain it to Bill. So I didn't bother. The last time I tried to explain things to Bill, I got all this psychology shit. Bill liked to think he could work me out. And sometimes I let him.

At least until the Wilfsberg ran out.

"So, how's it going down the pit?"

Misdirection. Like I cared. My dad, my granddad, my great granddad, they'd all gone down the pit. My great granddad died down there. It was a fucking hole.

"Not bad. The money's shit 'til I finish the apprenticeship. Then I'll be earning big time. Up to two hundred a week."

"Bollocks!"

"Yeah. The pit's a good earner. Not if you're like a rock ape, working the face. Any pleb can do that. But a sparks, that's different."

"Might be able to open your own brewery. Name in lights. 'Wilfsberg'... the pint that shrivels parts other beers cannot reach." Bill slapped me, playfully. But hard enough to hurt. As always. He loved me and Singe.

It was fucking embarrassing sometimes.

He got the Wilfsberg out and tested the temperature. Cold enough to cover the awkwardness. He filled our glasses and we sipped.

Vile puke shit.

If I could keep him drinking, he'd lay off with the nanny stuff. That was his only fault. And the fact that he wanked off his dog once. But today, not even the Wilfsberg could hold him back. It only encouraged him.

"You really should think about getting a trade."

Hurry up Singe. Rescue me with some wit or some inane shit.

"Singe is thinking about it. He's applied for a job at the airport. An apprenticeship. I think that's what he's gone home for now. To tell him."

"That should piss him off." Only the Army would get his son away from yobos like us. Well. Me. According to Singe's dad, everything wrong with the world was because they'd done away with National Service. Fucking Army. Making us into tidy, boot-licking, cannon fodder. Yeah. That's what the problem was. We needed another war. Get rid of some of the lay-about youth. Thin 'em out. Put 'em in the army! And those that came back home. Well, at least they'd have a trade. One armed, one-eyed, poppy-wearing flag wavers, employed on a

Sunday to worship the dead.

"I've got a trade."

Bill looked on. Waiting for the punchline.

"You're an artist, drawing the dole?" That passed for wit in Broadgate. I'd heard it so many times, my ears folded shut. Bill obviously had just discovered it. He was waiting for me to laugh.

"I'm a missionary." I said, straightly.

"From the bloody Milky Way."

I ran with it.

"I've come to save you all. Your planet is doomed."

Bill laughed. He'd not heard that one before. But I had.

I believed it once.

"When I was about five. I used to sit out front, waiting for them to come and pick me up, as I was sure I'd been dropped on the wrong planet."

This cracked Bill up. "You mad cunt."

If only I was. Mad. Life might be a bit simpler in some institution. Medication, mumbling and the occasional outburst and always, plans for escape. I shut down that mind wander before it made connections. More Wilfsberg. Liquid lobotomy needed. I knew what came next.

"You should talk to Fagg. Some of his mates teach in University." I don't know why he thought I should speak to them? Maybe they'd like to study me. Maybe he just wanted me to feel I was intelligent. Then I might pull out of my nosedive and get a trade instead of the crash and burn I was practicing.

Why did I need a job anyway? I was already going places.

I was a deep-sea diver.

Singe came back and saved me. Again. He looked a bit pissed off.

Really pissed off.

He looked like a kid who'd been crying.

"What's up?" said Bill pouring more Wilfsberg. He took it and sipped, without turning his nose up. Like something else inside was equally rotten.

"It's just my old man. I tried to tell him..."

Singe's bottom lip faltered.

"Just tell him what he wants to hear, then go for that job at the airport!"

Singe looked at Bill like he wanted to speak. But something had him by the throat.

"I can't talk to him about nothing."

Bill put his chunk arm around his shoulder and tipped the Wilfsberg glass to his lips. "You can talk to me about anything!"

I pulled a 'sick' face behind Bill's back and Singe laughed, wank-shitting his Wilfsberg.

Bill turned, but I dropped my face quicker than usual into neutral.

"Both of you can. You know that."

Singe used the choking laughter to cover his tears.

Bill missed it.

But I could smell the salt water. Her tears.

She was getting closer.

I changed the record, put The Pistols on for Singe.

From his pocket he produced three Tunal. Ace downers.

"Where'd you get them?"

"Leach. Apparently, his fat sister got anxiety attacks."

"Because she sold Leach all her slimming pills?" Bill chirped.

"Because she was just getting fatter and fatter and no one could work out why." Singe was always in fast. We cackled and slugged more Wilfsberg. Bill started explaining the lyrics of Bodies. About abortions in bags. We took one Tunal each. Bill declined, so Singe crushed it and put it into his glass without him noticing. Maybe that would shut him up.

Singe screamed the lyrics, releasing whatever had his throat in constriction.

Alone, taking a piss, I flashback.

Singe is not relaxing on a bed of small change, but sinking. His pupils replaced with perfectly round pennies.

I hope the Tunal kicks in soon.

It usually turns my head into a float.

Ça Plane Pour Moi

Heavy limbs. Heavy heads. Heated necks and fat lips. We were relaxed enough to get into Lords without scrutiny. Leach was at the door talking twelve to the dozen, trying to convince the bouncer to let him and his speeding friends in. He was looking thinner, older. Too old for this shit.

Inside the disco, the dance floor was empty. Dickie the DJ was still playing his beloved disco shit. No one, apart from Mongy John, the thirty-year-old mongoloid, was dancing. I danced with him, as I always did, while Singe and Bill got the soft drinks in. No alcohol in this bar tonight. Under eighteens present. Just pills and a bit of correction fluid being sucked in a dark corner by the glue boys. They'd left their Evo-stik behind tonight. Too smelly. But fluid was easy to smuggle in. A couple of drops on their jumper sleeves had them sucking like babies... until the buzz knocked them unconscious.

Dancing with Mongy John, I shuffled from side to side, my arms held flat against my body, shadowing his repetitive moves. He smiled his big innocent smile and gave me the thumbs up. In every youth club, Mongy John would be there. He always gave me the thumbs up as we danced. Everyone thought it was hilarious. Thought I was taking the piss. But I knew he was alright. In a place we couldn't be even with the drugs. He didn't care what we thought. He liked to dance, so he danced. If I wanted to dance I had to be pissed or pilled. So did most guys anywhere. The only thing I was ribbing was the music and Dickie the DJ. He was so in love with himself he thought it was him that got Mongy John Travolta up to dance!

Two girls from my old school saw me with John and knew the ritual.

They ran up screaming and danced either side. They were taking the piss, but did he care? John would be doing his happy little two-step while we got legless. Stumbled and tripped through our lives and fell into crippled normality.

We were the definitely the mongies, not John.

Another body lurched from the shadows around the dimly lit club. Bones, the Emmerdale Punk. He drove a tractor. His lanky frame swayed for a bit, trying to impersonate John. But he was obviously on something strong, as he tripped over and sprawled across the floor.

Leach and his speedy friends finally got in. They ran around the edge of the dance floor, trying to sell speed to everyone. Like a little swarm of mozzies. Another couple of Broadgate's misfits joined the Mongy dancing and Dickie had had enough.

"This one's for all you punks out there..."

'Ça Plane Pour Moi.'

Plastic Bertrand.

Cheese factor ten.

This was about as Punk as Dickie was going to get. He even sang the chorus to the girls from my old school. Michy had big tits. He'd like to get his hands on her. No chance. He was ten years older and even though he dressed in soul-boy slacks and wore plastic sandals, the girls still thought he was a twat. The only thing he got off with was his right hand.

Leach requested The Pistols. The Damned. 999. The Vibrators. X-ray Spex. The Clash. Sham 69.

Dickie put on Donna Summer. Punk Night? Spunk night!

Bill and Singe poured vodka into our lemonade. Bill's mum wouldn't miss it. She had a drinks cabinet, stacked. The band would be on later. The Crash Bats. What a shit name.

I looked at Singe. The Tunal was making his pupils large. Round. Penny-like. Full moon. Mind starting to stretch. Seeping out. I had to stop it before it rolled across the sand and got all mangled up in the surf.

Serious distraction needed.

Girls.

I spotted a few that needed avoiding. Not because they hated me. But because they wanted me. Again. I never went back to the same girl twice. Not a rule, just a habit. Didn't want to see what I'd left behind. I knew it was going to be a mess.

Jane. On the school playing field, during lunch break, as my mates played football. Jodie. I liked her and wanted to go back, but found Anne on the way home. I'd heard she'd been crying about it. She liked me too. But I couldn't even look back to wave. Then there was Carly. Rough. She wanked me off in the woods when I was fourteen. She was sixteen and was from a pikey family.

She was to be avoided at all costs. And her brothers.

Across the bar I saw Sue. Not the Fuzzy one, but the virginity one. I lost it to her when I was thirteen. She took me into her bedroom when I was playing with her little brother. We kissed on her bed. I got stiff and she helped me do the rest. She cocked the pistol but it was me who shot uncontrollably all over town. She had a boyfriend now. He was a bit hard. She smiled at me slyly while he wasn't looking. I turned. Eyes front. Shoulder back. On I went.

I saw her soon enough. My girl for the night. I knew her name was Lesley. She had long blonde hair and sweet eyes. Skinny arse and no tits. But her hair did it for me. Long and fair and lacquered flicks to the side. She was dancing with a friend that I knew. Fuzzy Sue's little sister, Sandy. I could get an intro. No problem. But I knew she'd make me dance with her. Fuck that. I'd wait.

I walked past a minute later and said hello to Sandy. Ignore. Ignore. Ignore. That was always the best way. I made sure I smiled at her as I walked away, to see if she was interested. She turned her head away, quickly. No eye contact. Okay. I'd work on it. At least she'd seen me.

I rejoined Singe and Bill at the table in a dark corner. The Soul Boys were coming in. Older than us. Some of them were on the fringe of the Rent-a-Riot lot. Tatts, gold belcher chains. Sovereign rings. Knock-off Farrah trousers and La Coste sports shirts. They'd come in to pick up the younger birds. The bouncers had no problems with that.

Now it was even. The punks and the soul boys filled Lords fifty-fifty.

The crackle started to build. Hormone static. Dickie was in his element. Playing disco tunes to piss us off, now his 'fans' were there. Standing around the edge of the dance floor, swaggering, swaying, beery-cheery. They hated the Punks more than the Teds or the Hippies or the Rockers. They told us their dads fought the war for people like us. I never got what they meant. I thought they fought the war because they had to. For themselves.

They tried to be patriotic. It made them idiotic.

The country was fucked. We all were.

What really pissed me off about them was the soul boys were the biggest supporters of the National Front. Football-loving fuckwits who didn't like the fact that the country was changing. 'Send them back! Send the coons back!' They wanted an England that ruled the world. A Britannia that ruled the waves.

That was what was wrong with them. Arrogant enough to think someone could rule the waves!

They couldn't even hold their beer!

Dickheads.

One of them would dance soon. If they didn't smack a fist into a face first.

Bones was staggering to some inaudible beat. He was gone. Falling into tables and generally being drunk. Bones was taller than all the soul boys. It wouldn't be him.

The tension held for now.

Four or five girls bopped to one side, with Mongy John, including Lesley. She was trying to act cool, sipping her drink through a straw, head bent, eyes peeping from under the lacquered hair, looking for someone. Me?

I made sure she saw me as I skirted the dance floor, weaving in and out between the soul boys. Minding their pints held proud. The match to light the fuse.

Lesley saw me and turned to dance with John. She was doing a shit job of ignoring me.

In the bog, I stood next to Danny at the pisser. A soul boy I knew from school. A right prick. I'd heard he'd been going with Lesley for a while.

"Alright?"

"What's this Punk Night all about?"

"There's a band on in a minute."

I'd be glad to finish this piss. You can't fight with your cock out. Unless you're cock fighting.

"Punk Night? Nobody wants that, do they."

"It's just a laugh."

C'mon finish pissing before him. Nope. He's shaking and zipping already. Filling his pint of coke with brandy from a hip flask.

"You havin' a laugh?"

Conversation sliding dangerously towards "Are you laughing at us, me, etc." Deflection needed.

"Plenty of girls here though."

His beer-brain bounced.

"Yeah. Fucking birds everywhere."

Pissing finished. Bolder now. Hands free.

"Are you still going with that blonde girl?" Pretending not to know her name.

"Lesley? Nah, fucking slag two-timed me."

Good news. probably tired of being his trinket. That's the type they all wanted. Trinket girls. Dangling. Shiny. Obedient. Girls that protected them from their greatest fear - the gay slur. If they had a bird, they couldn't be gay. That made them 'straight'. NF straight. Punch your bird in the face straight.

"Don't get too pissed."

"Try not to."

Ha ha. Plastic laughs. That's exactly what we'd both do. But a few more snide drinks and he'd be trying to prove what a hard, straight bloke he was. He'd fail to get off with a bird and start a fight.

Wanker. But his loss was my gain.

Lesley was available.

I wanted her more now than ever. I wanted to take her away from all this shite and fuck her, freeing myself from this boredom. Massive boredom. Drink. boredom. Drugs. Boredom. Family. Boredom. Dole. Boredom. Sex... that at least, was still a non-boring option.

The one time I felt connected.

Engaged. In free flow.

On the dance floor we arrived back together. Now she saw me with her ex. No turning away. I ducked past Bones and started to dance with her. She smiled at Danny. Little knife smile. Stab stab cut. He turned, bleeding, to the bar.

"You been speaking to Danny?" She shouted above the music.

"Yeah."

"What'd he say about me?"

"Nothing."

"Anyway, he's a fucking liar."

The music stopped abruptly. Her last word 'liar' travelled well. He heard it. Liar.

Slight.

Might be gay.

Liar.

Danny stared across at me. Match lit, held below the tip of his fag. He lit it and took a drag. Blowing smoke away he turned back to the drink on the bar. His mate looked at him. What? What's the problem?

Maybe he'd heard about my brother.

No problem. More drink.

His fuse was lit but still burning. Slowly.

Not yet.

At school, he'd always wanted to have a pop at me, but Bill was in the wings, waiting. He knew he'd have to fight him as well. That was enough. But I knew he hated me. I'd seen it in his eyes when he'd walk past me at lunch time. I was talking to the girls, and he didn't know how. Now he'd have to think twice about starting on me because Martin had thrashed all their best men.

Advantage psycho brother.

Lesley was on.

"You wanna walk home with me later?" Code for 'come into the school playing fields near your house and drop your knickers.'

"You don't live near me." She smiled and sipped through the straw. That was a definite yes.

"See ya later."

Nothing more to do or say. Just make sure I left at the same time as Sandy to walk them home.

Dickie interrupted with perfect timing, for a twat.

"Now, what you've all been waiting for. Well, some of you. Let's hear you give a big Lord's welcome to... The Crash Bats."

The sticky-backed plastic, 'here's one I made earlier' Blue Peter punk band strutted onto stage. The lead guitarist, some middle-class guy called Mark, scowled, trying to look disinterested. All Johnny Rotten. But I saw how much he wanted us to like him. He opened with, "We're the Crash Bats. If you don't like it, you can fuck off." The Soul Boys jeered. The punks cheered and rushed the dance floor as the band began thrashing a Rolling Stones cover to bits.

Satisfaction.

The band was worse than shit. At least it was enough to ruin the Soul Boys' night. They started to leave as the punks pogoed and flung each other around.

I sat back with Bill and Singe. Singe was too wankered to get up. Bill was minding him.

"Where were you?"

Singe obviously had more pills but wasn't sharing. His massive pupils floated in his eyes like rubber rings in a pool.

Bill slapped him across the cheek.

Singed groaned like a dog shitting billiard balls.

"He's out of it."

"He'll be alright."

"No he fucking won't. We've got to get him home."

"Just leave him. He's listening to the band."

Singe rolled his eyes and echoed me poorly.

"Listening to the band." His head collapsed onto the table. "Are they on yet?"

I laughed. Bill, who was well Wilfed, threw up his hands and went for a piss. The band played another song. I think they had six on their set list. I could see it stuck to a little monitor at the front of the low stage.

The song was crap. I couldn't hear much of it, but I think it was something about fighting the police. Ha! I knew their front man was from the posh end of town. The only time he'd met the police was when they stopped him for having no lights on his chopper. Still, there was a good buzz in the club now. We were taking over for the first time. The Soul Boys were pushed to the sides and we were centre stage. Trampy bunch of nowhere kids. Scrap heap scrappers, having their say. Nothing to say, but saying it loud and proud anyway.

Must have been the Tunal. I was loved up. Part of the crowd. If Singe would have been conscious we'd have been pogoing with the rest of them.

Imitating what we'd seen on TV and read in the papers. Punk had given flamethrowers to a bunch of pyromaniacs and the chance to burn this disco down.

I spotted Lesley at the bar speaking to Danny. Then arguing with Danny. She walked away, grabbing Sandy by the arm. Was she leaving? Must find out. Singe was puking. I couldn't leave him and follow. Held his head over the side of the table. He mumbled through spit.

"I love you."

Yeah. Love you too.

Lesley was definitely leaving. She did a circuit of the dance floor holding her coat. Took a sip of her almost empty drink and tried not to look my way.

An invite I couldn't ignore.

Bill arrived in the nick of time. I rested Singe's head on his arm across the table.

"Keep an eye on him. I'm going outside. Need some fresh air." Bill glared at me. "Your brother's outside, asking for you."

Shit.

"What's he want?"

"I dunno. Let's take Singe home." Bill tried to lift him. He was a dead weight. "Grab his arm."

Singe started resisting and raving.

"Can't take him up like this. The bouncers will call the Old Bill. Take him to the toilet." Bill agreed. We dragged him around the quietest route to the bogs.

Danny stood in our way.

"Give him some more glue."

"Fuck off Danny." Bill was taking no prisoners. Danny tried to laugh it off and held a drink out to Singe. Mocking the afflicted.

"Want a little drinky?"

Singe saw the pint dangling and flayed his arms, spasmodically, swimming towards it. He slipped through me and flopped to the floor. Groping Bill's leg he pulled himself to a sitting position.

Danny offered the drink again. Same joke, same stupid laughter.

Bill pushed him away.

"What d'ya do that for. Prick. I was only having a laugh."

"Not funny, you cunt. Fuck off." Bill was in fighting mode. He kicked Singe from around his leg and stepped, squared shouldered, towards Danny. His two Soul Boy mates closed in behind.

This was it. Fight or flight.

Lesley was getting away.

Bones came to the rescue. Stumbling backwards from the dance floor, he tripped and lost control. Smacking into Danny.

Both ended in a heap. But Bones kept on dancing. Pulling Danny to his feet, laughing, making him pogo with him. The Soul Boys pushed and prized him away and span Bones back onto the dance floor.

Bill picked up Singe.

"No need to fight over me girls," he slurred, "you can ALL take me home."

The anger paused. Singe wobbled into the bogs with Bill. More puking. This time in the big white bowl invented for it.

"I'm going to see what my brother wants, outside."

Bill didn't protest. He was beyond it now. His temper cooling to a white heat. He would wait for Danny to come in.

Danny was going to get it.

I left him to it.

Outside, the smell of the incoming tide rinsed the harbour air with seaweed, mud and diesel. Above, the full moon pulled people this way and that. But always to the seafront. To the seashore. Waves of people rolled along the street washing against the pubs and breaking into groups, foaming at the mouth. Looking for something to down.

To drown.

I looked for Lesley. I needed dry land.

Which way had she gone?

I traced her in my mind. Up Harbour Street. Through the centre of town she'd be trotting on platformed feet. Tottering on past the shops, the church, the streets getting narrower. Past the stacks of terraced houses, sliding down the hill into each other, like bowed bread slices.

Sandy would say goodnight at the entrance to the little street that ran west, out to the mud flats and nothing. The playing fields by the school came next. Then Lesley's home. One in the middle of six. By a parade of shops. Then Seddington. No-go for my flow. I had to get to her before the playing fields. Or it was a walk all the way back into town and then east along the clifftop, through the park. Seddington sprawled all the way to the railway track and I didn't fancy being chased over that again.

I looked both ways, but this time looking to avoid my brother.

Across the road, towards Harbour Street. Quick step. Don't run. Don't stand out. Go with the flow. Swim with the shoal.

"Oi! Jimmy!"

Shit. Brother.

"Where you going at double time?"

"Home."

"That's up that way." His eyes seemed nervous. Quieter. Younger.

"I'm getting some chips."

"I'll come with ya."

Fuck. Just tell him. Can't. Don't want him in on anything. This is my chase.

"Why were you looking for me?"

March in step. Hup two. Three four. Chip shop. Stop.

"I wanted to borrow some money."

Money. Pocket. Yes. "Why haven't you got any?"

"Army cocked up. They're sending me a new cheque. Next week."

Lie in the eye. But mine were focused elsewhere. Up the road. Lesley and Sandy over the hill to home.

"How much do you want?"

"How much you got?"

Funny answer. Pockets rustle. Two screwed up pound notes. The last of my dole money. "It's all I've got."

Martin takes it and smiles. "You'll get it back."

"Yeah. See ya later."

I'm marching again. Trying to stop my legs from running. Martin calls out after me.

"Cheers."

Chip shop shut. All shops shut. He drops out of sight. I start to run.

Black windows flashing by. Bins spilling over, robbed by seagulls.

Top of town. Fewer people. Then down.

No people.

No Lesley.

Running. Love the way my heavy legs roll like lead weights swinging under me. Dr. Marten's cushioning the pavement's blow.

Sandy's street. Brakes on full. She's at the gate. Talking. Now, keep out of sight. Get breath. Think of excuse. Got it. Looking for brother. Told me to meet him somewhere around.

Lesley is surprised to see me.

"What you doing up here?"

"Walking this way. My brother, Martin, wants me to meet him up Seddington."

"What's he doing, looking for someone?"

"Maybe? I can walk you home now. It's up that way isn't it?"

As if I didn't know. I'd seen her leaving her house when I went to meet my dad on a building site next to the school. I remembered the hair. No hair spray but still the colour of wheat before burning. Sunny. Warm. Inland. I loved the smell of it. Straw to roll in and rub ourselves against while we kissed. Dry, sweet, but fucking itchy if it got down your pants.

Lesley walked. I followed.

I moved alongside her and put my arm around her waist. She did the same and we bumped our hips playfully. Another good sign. Her house was within spitting distance. The hole in the fence leading to the school field was looming.

I stopped and turned her towards me. She smiled, knowing what came next. I kissed her. She kissed back. Hot, wet kiss. Big mouth for a skinny girl. Her tits were tight in her top. Hard nipples. I was soon boned-up.

"I'm not going in there with you."

Act surprised. Kiss her again.

"I'm not a slag."

"I know."

Try to kiss again and feel tits. Hands deflected.

"I know what you're like."

"What?"

"As soon as you've fucked me, you'd be gone. On to the next one."

I couldn't lie. Why bother?

"You've got a reputation."

I liked that. A bit. I laughed.

Rumbled.

I was led by the hand past the hole in the fence. Lesley smiling all the way, to her doorstep. The kissing was getting more intense. That was good, but my cock was aching now. I had to get something.

"Wanna come in, for a coffee."

"I'll nick one of your dad's beers."

"My dad's in ya know."

I shrug my shoulders. So what? I'm innocent.

Her key comes out and she quietly opens the door to the little terraced cottage. The kitchen lies beyond the front room. The door is shut. Sounds of TV inside. We make it to the kitchen undetected. Lesley goes for the kettle. I grab her and push her against the cupboard. Kissing is even harder. We're both breathing gentle breaths, soft as a horse's nostril.

I pull her arse towards me with both hands, pressing my cock into her. She grinds against it and moans.

Quietly.

She suddenly breaks away and opens the serving hatch to the front room.

"Hello. Wanna cuppa?"

Muffled replies. Not really. Mum's asleep, Dad dozing watching TV. She shuts the thin wooden partitions and smiles at me coolly. "Wanna see my bedroom?"

I don't. I don't wanna be trapped upstairs, with her dad standing at the bottom, blocking my exit.

"Let's stay here."

She's confused.

I can see the back door.

My escape.

I advance, slowly. I stroke her hair, give her my 'special' look. I mean it right now. I've never wanted anyone so much in this moment, before. That makes her special.

Bluff needed.

I kiss her affectionately on the cheek and put the kettle on.

I pass the test. She puts her arms over my shoulders and kisses my neck. I turn into her and see it in her eyes.

She's mine.

For one night.

One moment.

I start with her buttons and zip, fumbling like a child with his hand in a bag of marbles. She stops me and I pull her flares down over her sweet little arse. "Come upstairs," she whispers. I ignore her and push her down onto the long wooden bench by the breakfast table. I lay her back gently and she smiles, rebelliously. She lifts her hips and her jeans roll down past her knees, then one leg is free and wraps around my thighs. I unzip and push my cock towards her. She helps by pulling her knickers aside. We fuck like little bolters. Glancing towards the serving hatch, I strain. Listening for movement. Intoxicated by the danger, we plough on. I have to be quick.

"Don't come in me."

"I won't."

I can't. Against my rules. No pregnancy. I couldn't be tied down with a ball and chain like that. Smash it, run and don't look back.

But this is good. I don't want to run, I want to be there at the end, when the Old Bill turn up and nick me. I wanna be caught.

Fucking weird.

I thrust harder. I'm going to come in her. She rows back with her hips. Deeper. Faster. I start to lose control. She pushes back with her hands on my shoulders. I lean all my weight forward and explode into her. Collapsing. Falling. Running headlong, like some berserker, screaming but biting my tongue.

Then the sea. Washing over my dead body. Waves rocking me gently back and forth until they withdraw, dumping me on the warm sand.

She pulls me down and kisses me.

"You bastard."

"Don't worry. You won't get pregnant."

"How do you know?"

"I Just do."

I see the look jump from her lips to eyes, riding her wry smile.

She wants to be pregnant.

She thinks she's got me.

But I see her one month on. Pursed lips that won't tell me she's come on again. She'll try and string it out. She wants control. Not over me.

Just over her own little bit of life. She really wants to worry Danny. Tell him it could be his. Then tell him the kid's not his, when she's had enough of him.

So fucked up.

I kiss her goodbye. I'm out the door. She says, "Do you want to go out with me?"

"Maybe." Means no.

"I'm going down town tomorrow. Meet me."

"Yeah. Ok."

I walk. I look back for once. She's smiling. She thinks I'm attached. Good try. But you're not going to be preggers. I know. I would have seen it coming. I feel things, see things, when I come.

It's the sea.

The fucking wet stuff again.

I wave goodbye. Won't be seeing Lesley too soon. Not even when this little bit of wheat needs re-sowing.

Orgasm Addict

A good night. The stars are out. The sky is empty of clouds.

I walk through the streets, alone with my breath and footsteps echoing. Past the silent cemetery. I reach the top of the hill. The Old Bill drive past. Slowly. I don't look. I come from Prestwell. We all look guilty to them.

Some of us are.

They speed up and fuck off. Even better. I stop and sit on a low wall. What a night.

Buzzing.

Got away with it again.

The Milky Way is clear above me.

I'm right up there with it. In dry space, where nothing can touch me. Footsteps in the alley across the road. I recognise that swaying silhouette. Dad?

I catch his 'drinking shirt' under the street lamp. Definitely Dad. He doesn't spot me, so, in good spirits, I jump over the cemetery wall. I'm gonna scare the shit out of him when he walks past at the other end.

The drop on the other side is higher. My ankle twists. Fuck. Pain. By the time I get to my feet, he's almost down the road. If I'm quick I can cut him off before he crosses to the corner and hits Prestwell.

I hobble as fast as I can. Pain drains. I speed up. I leap up onto the wall. But I'm too late, he's already crossed. But not into Prestwell. He's turned right, down Shilby Avenue. Into the posh houses.

I drop onto the grey pavement and follow.

Like a commando, I stalk the enemy, in silence. Brushing privet hedges and diving into lavender cover, I get close enough to hear him humming. A series of unconnected notes. Like the ones he makes when he's shaving in the kitchen and Mum, spitting, is in the living room ironing his drinking shirt.

He's on it. The scent. I know that smell.

He turns into a little cul-de-sac and it becomes crystal. The street lamp on the fritz winks as he passes under it.

Auntie Joy.

Now it clicks. Why their 'arguments' get so heated.

The dirty fucker.

He sways to the front door, but then, even in his pissed-up state, he remembers. Tap tap tap ta-tap tap tap on the window. Like the little tuneless tune he was humming.

A curtain swishes. The door opens quickly. She protests in a whisper. I can imagine. He's about as discreet as a tom cat pissing up a post.

I go to the window and listen. I cannot hear anything above choking American pop slush. I doubt for a minute. Perhaps he's just finishing their latest debate. I cannot be sure.

Oh yes I can.

The back gate is open. But the back door locked.

Shit.

I must find another way in. The kids' window is open above the flat roof extension. Up I go, like Spiderman. My arm reaches through and pops the large window. It glides open, net curtains wafting me with warm sick-kid and clean bedroom smell. Her two boys, Barry and Davy, asleep, wrapped in hot duvet safety.

I step carefully over the older one's bed. The creaking boards don't wake them.

I'm out into the hall. Bright. Their little sister sleeps with the light on. It's hard to make the Muppet out amongst the cuddly toys. I pull her door to.

Dark means quiet.

Auntie's bedroom. Very quiet. Too quiet. Pitch black. They're downstairs in case they wake the kids with their grunting.

The stairs are fucking noisy. Each step sounds like I'm squashing bullfrogs. My heart revs, ready to bolt if that front room door opens.

The landing, front door, soft carpet. I hold the door handle. Sweat on cheap metal. What am I gonna do? Jump in and shout 'BOO!'

I push my ear against the door. I can hear the distinctive sound of naked flesh rubbing on leather-look furniture. I'm not sure I really wanna see that. Auntie Joy spread beneath him on the sofa. Them wrestling like mating squid.

She starts moaning out loud. In time with the soft soundtrack to their movie.

'Ah-ah-aaa afternoon delight!'

Mind fuck.

I hope she's got her teeth in. I couldn't help but imagine.

Why scar myself like that?

I'm sick.

I bolt upstairs. This time, jumping from the bed onto the windowsill. I drop onto the roof and roll. Then walk out front, slamming the gate as hard as I can.

I look back and see the curtain swish.

Who cares?

Fancy cheating on Mum. With that. Two-faced bitch.

I sat on a lawn at the end of the sac. Then laid back to stare at infinity.

My anger subsided.

I smiled a little secret smile to the stars. He had some front! Then I thought of Mum, lying there, always asleep on the sofa, worn out, practically dead. I became angry again.

What would I do about it? What could I do about it?

I wouldn't get married and have kids for a start.

I glanced back at my 'great night out' and turned away, twice as quickly.

Is this all there is?

Is that what I had to look forward to in this prison? Marrying someone from the same town and producing sprog after sprog? Bouncing up and down until her stretch marks catapulted me off down the road onto the sofa of a toothless divorcee, for a bit of 'Afternoon Delight'.

Vomit.

The blinking street lamp gave up with a dull click. I could see space emerging above, beneath, around me. Some cosmic tide washing. Sloshing.

I let myself float for just a moment.

Just a stupid, heart-cracked moment.

The question slips out.

"There must be more to life than this?"

Fatal.

I am ready.

Finished.

I hear a rumble in the distance. Like a stampede coming or an earthquake.

No. A tidal wave.

Cause made. Effect inevitable.

No escape.

This is my vision. This is what I've seen.

The answer to my stupid question is coming to get me.

Liquid.

To fill an empty vessel.

The Eve Of Destruction

In my house, no matter what shit happens, everything will be alright. It has to be. Not that my mum and dad know what they're doing. They don't. But when the Old Bill come calling, it's never as bad as I think it's going to be with them, in fact, it almost seems like it's a relief. Like they know they're living up to their necks in shit and the pigs are doing them a favour pushing their heads under. Yeah, I get it in the neck for a day or two. But they just forgive me. Like they've been expecting it all their lives.

At school, when I beat up a couple of twats, for calling my mum a whore, and then smashed the gym to pieces, I was hauled in front of the headmaster. My dad went in with me.

"You are a disgrace to this school, etc. We don't expect you to behave like a thug."

Then my dad gets up and starts giving it the finger. The pointy one that always makes him right.

"Wait a minute, the other boys weren't innocent in all this."

Major shock. The headmaster wouldn't be questioned and went into one. A moral rant. His Church of England School was above all this. My dad didn't like being talked down to and I slipped off the hook as they argued.

I left the school with its smart badge and middle class aspirations and went to the local comprehensive. Much better. Nobody looking at me. When I wanted to pop up and do some work, the teachers enjoyed my attention. We were all part of some educational experiment and they were glad to have a few lab rats running round the maze the right way for a change.

When the MPs came calling, looking for Martin, the atmosphere was on parade, but I watched Mum and Dad deal with it in their usual way. Denial. When the two suited geezers left, carrying their red hats politely under the arm of their washed out, rainy day uniforms, the silence was broken by Dad.

"He must have had a reason. He wouldn't have just left."

Yeah, a reason. People don't just act like idiots. They have to have a reason. "Maybe it was being passed over for promotion."

Sure. He'd wanted to join the SAS, but he was too noisy. They only liked quiet killers. Maybe it was because he was a mad fucker who didn't like being told what to do? I saw it in his eyes. Rent-a-Riot tried to beat him down, to make him comply. He wasn't having that. Nobody was telling him what to do.

My mum sat and smoked her second cigarette. "You don't think he's really in trouble?"

"Course he's in trouble. He's gone AWOL. When they catch him they'll chuck him in the glass house."

"How long will he be locked up for?"

"Depends what he did with his kit."

"What kit?"

"His kit. His army issue. Boots, webbing. That sort of thing."

"Not his gun?"

"No. Not his gun. He'll get three years if he has."

"I don't think Martin would do anything like that..."

Her voice tailed off as she sucked on the ciggie. For once, it wasn't going to be alright and they knew it. What a relief. At last the shit was going to hit the fan. Bullseye!

But what shit?

I left them swirling in their guilt vortex and went upstairs to figure things out. Martin hadn't been around the house since yesterday lunchtime. The last time I saw him was outside Lords, when he lent money from me. Bullshit story about the army pay. That's why he wanted it. He wasn't on leave, he was on the run.

My heart picked up the pace a bit. My brain started to sprint. He must have at least shot someone, stolen a tank, set fire to the officers' mess.

I needed to get out. Breakfast. Clothes. My mind was all over the place. I was rooting around the floor for a clean t-shirt when I stopped. Rigid.

Under my bed, something was missing.

My fucking airgun.

He'd sold his gun, now he was trying to sell mine. Bastard.

I had to find him.

Still dressing, I jumped over the back fence and headed up the alley. I wanted to check out Beanie's. At the back gate I peered at the windows. No lights on downstairs. Beanie's mum never let anyone stay. She never let anyone in. Since her husband went mad, she kept everything locked away. Tight. Kitchen knives especially. Martin told me that Beanie used to eat his tea with plastic ones, just in case.

Martin wouldn't be there.

The garden shed was falling down. The roof felt ripped and the door hanging off its hinges. Not a good hiding place. Should I go and knock for Beanie? He might know something. Was it too early? What day was it? I went round the side of the house and looked up at Beanie's window. Tommy David and his wife were off down the street. He had his neck brace on. She wore makeup and her best coat. Off to the pub to spend a bit of dole money. He couldn't work because he'd hurt his neck. Didn't stop him tilting his head back for the pints to go down. So my Dad always said, jealously, as they came back again after three, red-faced and talking loudly, laughing. Carried on a full sail of piss and wind.

So, it was Saturday. Just before twelve. You could set your watch by Mr. and Mrs. David.

It was late enough not to rile his mum, or his dad, if he was home from the loony bin. I knocked at the door. No answer. I thought I heard a broken voice shouting 'go away'. A door closed inside. Someone moved towards me. The net curtain wiped the dirty glass on the front door. Beanie's little sister answered. She was cute. But only twelve. And a bit ginger.

"Yeah?"

"Beanie in?"

"Yeah."

"Can you get him for me?"

"What for?"

"I wanna speak to him." Best smile. She scowls. Like a little bitch. Trying to act older.

"Why?"

"Just get him."

She slams the door shut in my face. She likes me. I've seen her and her little mates playing out on the Green when I walk by. They dare each other to chuck stuff or say stuff. She always puts them up to it. Wanting my attention.

She'll get him for me.

A few seconds pass and the window opens above. It's Beanie, looking half asleep or stoned, as usual. I know he hasn't seen Martin. I can tell. But I ask him anyway. I want to share my excitement with someone.

"Seen Martin?"

"Nah. Not for a while, I think. Why? What's he been up to?"

"He's gone AWOL."

"Shit!"

"Yeah. Big shit."

"Yeah. Big, big shit. When did he run?"

"I don't know. The MPs came today. This morning."

"Shit."

"Yeah."

"Shiiiiit!"

"I bet he's already left the country."

Beanie laughs. Delighted. "Fucking yeah. Probably in France or, somewhere." Couldn't think of another country. Spent too much time on the weed. "If you see him, yeah," he raises a clenched fist, "tell 'im, rock on!"

I didn't bother returning the gesture. "Rock on!" Where the fuck did that come from? The middle finger. Two fingers would do, but rock on? Cock on! I think he'd been listening to too much David Essex.

Gypsy tart.

I was just about two doors away when the mad screaming of a moped on full throttle came round the bend in the avenue. Then, tyres screeching. Skidding. It was Little Frank, a thief of the Sanders clan who loved mopeds.

"Jimmy!"

"Alright?"

Maybe he'd seen my brother. Maybe he had a message from him.

"What ya doing?"

He hadn't. Nothing doing. His face was the same as always, wide-eyed and dangerous. Buzzing from the stolen bike. "Wanna ride?"

I jumped on. He was always good for a lift. I wanted to get to Singe's. Quick. The only trouble with getting a lift with Little Frank is that nine times out of ten you'd get a police escort. It wasn't long before the poxy Panda was after us. If it had been a Jam Sandwich we'd have been nicked in no time. But even the little 50cc could outrun the Panda, especially down the alley that led to the Old Park.

We jumped off, the bike still running. Frank rolled it into the brambles.

"See ya later Jimmy."

"Cheers for the lift, Frank the wank."

The sole occupant of the Panda was puffing down the road after. On foot. So, I made tracks into the deep tangles of bracken and blackberry at the edge of the wood. The Old Park had at least half an acre of overgrown to hide in. Plus a few big gardens that backed onto it. Over them and I'd be back in Prestwell in time for World of Sport.

I ducked into the grass and bracken, then crawled commando style to the tree line. I could hear the copper's walkie-talkie. More were coming. A meat wagon pulled into the avenue along the edge of the park. They really wanted Frank this time. It was probably his second or third of the day. Thieving little bastard.

The fat pig from the Panda was walking towards my position, edging the long grass and brambles. His route would cross the small mud path that ran behind me, into a clearing in the wood we called the toad hole.

I crawled backwards into the trees. I could easily make it out of the wood I knew so well and over the road, across the gardens and home. Behind a small oak, I stood up, ready to run.

A hand clamped down over my mouth. Another held me firmly by the shoulder. I didn't bolt. I knew it wasn't the pigs. The hand released itself slowly from my mouth as Martin's mud-streaked face pushed in close. He silenced me with a finger and led me quietly away through the wood.

In a dense shit of hawthorn and elderberry, he pulled me down into a bracken-covered ditch. Hidden by sticks, invisible from the outside.

He waited until the pig withdrew from the wood and whispered. "Those idiots won't find us here."

A sleeping bag lay on a sheet of builder's plastic. A bottle of water and my airgun. Easy to pack away into his bergen.

"What the fuck are you doing here, with my airgun?"

"Survival."

"Surviving what?"

"If they catch me I'll do time. I'm not being banged up again. I went AWOL."

"I know. The MPs have been round."

"What did they say?"

Eyes supremely animated. Predator sharp.

"Nothing much. Just asked if we'd seen you?"

"And?"

"Mum said you hadn't been home for a few days."

I picked up my gun. He took it straight back.

"I've borrowed it."

"What you going to do now? Have you got a plan?"

Army people in my films always had a plan.

"Dunno. Need money. Maybe leave the country and join the Legion."

"Foreign Legion?"

"Yep. No questions asked."

"Can't you just get your kit and give it back to the Army?"

Martin thought about this one and smiled.

"Not possible."

We sat in silence for a moment, listening to the birds, the wind in the trees. I checked the cops. The Panda car had gone. But the meat wagon stayed. The two pigs sparked up and started talking. The chase for Frank and me was over. For now.

Martin relaxed and rummaged in his bergen. A small backy tin. Inside, an eighth of gold. He rolled a joint and offered some to me. I declined. Martin gazed across the smoke as it tumbled through the beams of daylight and away to nowhere. A pigeon landed in the tall tree above. Martin picked up the gun and cocked it slowly.

The barrel clicked coldly back into place. There was already a pellet in the breech.

He took aim. Bang. I thought he'd never hit it from that distance. A loud, feather-softened thud followed. A thrashing of wings and the struggling bird fell down through the canopy. By the time I got through the undergrowth it was almost dead. I picked it up. Martin pointed the reloaded barrel and shot it through the head as I held it. A small spot of blood spattered onto my lip.

I offered the bird up to him.

"Put it in my camp. I need a few more."

Martin crept away into the woods to hunt and I tossed the pigeon through the stick and bracken arch into his hideout. Then I just stood there.

Fuck. I was actually scared. If I got caught with him, would I get banged up? When was I getting my gun back? Fuck the gun, he could have it. I went to tell him.

Following the pneumatic crack of a shot being fired off, I found him in the darkest part of the wood. I didn't like it there. Always felt like something was watching with big, slow eyes. It was always quieter than the rest of the wood. Still. Damp. An air of living decay sucked slowly on everything.

Fungal.

Brackish.

Martin had a blackbird hanging from his belt and was taking aim at something else. My foot pushed a rotting twig down into the moss.

A moist snap.

I saw a collared dove breaking for open sky. Wings wheezing as they thrashed it to safety. He glared at me. "You scared it."

"I just came to tell ya, you can keep the gun."

A superior smile.

"Cheers."

I turned to retrace my steps.

"Don't tell anyone I'm here..."

I shook my head and kept walking. Imagining him pointing the rifle at the back of my head as I retreated.

"And bring me some bread and shit. I'm fucking starving."

Fuck. Now I'd have to come back.

"Tonight."

Suspect Device

A loaf of bread, a tin of beans and some milk. I tried to hide them in the cupboard under the sink as Mum came in.

"Going shooting. Tonight. I needed some supplies."

She took them and stuck them back in the larder.

"There's a pork pie and some crisps in the bread bin. I was saving the beans for your father. But he's done his usual."

He was out on the piss. Maybe shagging Auntie Joy again. There would be a big fight later. There always was. I remember the time Mum smashed the burglar stick over his head and the police came. Took him away. I was about five. The police scared me. I didn't want them to take my dad away. But he'd been threatening to take pills. They were scattered all over the living room carpet. The empty brown bottle laying on its side, like a dead soldier.

"Thanks Mum."

I took the food and a torch. Its batteries were running out by the time I'd crossed over the long grass into the wood. Dim grey light just made the track visible. I was more scared now than ever. I sat in the graveyard, on my own, without fear. But that was because nobody was there. I knew somebody was here.

Waiting. For me.

With plans.

I stepped deeper into the trees, hoping for just a tick, that the pigs had found him. A hope in vain. The glow of a camp fire sent streaks of shadow through the trees and lit the bottom of shimmering leaves, making them autumnal before their time. Martin was waiting for me by his den, standing back in the shadows, away from the fire. He took the bag from me and we sat. On opposite sides of the fire. He looked at the pork pie and crisps and put them back into the carrier.

"Where's the milk? The bread?"

"Mum caught me. I didn't want her to get suspicious."

"Good work. Don't worry about the milk. I'll nick some from the doorsteps."

Silence. Fire crackle.

Downy breast feathers caught in the firelight seemed to be floating above the dark earth. Above the ivy-covered floor. A tawny owl shrieked. I scanned the black canopy. Nothing. I was glad. He couldn't shoot what he couldn't see. My eyes came back. Martin stared across the fire. Checking me. Sizing me up for his plans. Would he kill me and bury me in the toad hole now I'd discovered him? Was bringing food a test? He tossed me the bag of crisps and then munched into the pork pie. I kept looking for the owl. I thought I glimpsed it on the dead branch, silhouetted against the light-polluted sky.

"It's okay. There's no one out there."

"I was just looking for the owl."

"Can't eat it. Did you tell anyone else? Your mates?"

"Nah. Don't be stupid!"

"Good. I need time."

"What for?"

"To get money."

"To join the Legion?"

"Maybe."

It was so quiet I could hear his jaw clicking as he ate the pie. Green twigs hissed in the fire, spitting sap. Something tiny rustled the leaves behind me. My heart gulped. I had to get out. Now.

"Your mate..."

"Singe?"

"Yeah. Singe. He's always up for it, right?"

"Up for what?"

"A laugh."

A laugh as in, I'm punching you as hard as I can in the guts, but it's only a laugh. A bully's excuse.

"Yeah. He's a mad fucker."

"He's got a bike, right?"

"I think he smashed it up."

Lie.

"Shit."

"He's alright."

"What?"

"He didn't get smacked up. Just totalled the bike."

"Yeah? How badly?"

"Dunno. Write off, I think." What the fuck did he want with Singe's bike? Probably thinking of 'borrowing' that too.

"Good that he didn't get smacked up. I might need another man."

Another man! Fuck! We're both part of his plan.

"I need some money to get to Paris, to the Legion's recruiting centre. I can't hitchhike in case I get picked up. I'm going to rob the amusements. On the seafront. Are you in?"

Like Flynn.

"We've been robbing that place forever."

Banging the penny falls. Blowing silver fag paper across the lines of the 'wheel 'em in'. Usually just enough to get a bag of chips to prolong the day at the beach.

"I'm gonna wait a couple of weeks, 'til the summer's over. They keep the takings in a safe, in the office. They'll be more money then."

"A safe? How you going to get into that?"

A big goofy smile. He reached back into the den and dragged his bergen to the fire. He rummaged and threw something across the flames. I caught it. It's heavy and cold. Metal.

"A fucking hand grenade! Where d'ya get that?"

Stupid question.

"The army lent me it."

Stupid answer.

I was grinning like a trippy twat. He'd got me.

"We can blow the safe up. It's meant to be a shite one."

I tossed the grenade from hand to hand. It wasn't the first time I'd handled one. I was ten. A kid brought a deactivated World War Two example into school. I wanted it so much that I stole it. The teacher did that thing. Y'know, 'I'm going to leave the classroom door open during lunch, so the person who took it could put it back... where it belongs...' I felt so guilty, that I did. And he didn't bother pulling me up for stealing it in the first place. That grenade was inert. Inactive.

This one was live. A total buzz.

Martin snatched it back.

"Don't worry, you'll get to pull the pin." The grenade went back into the bergen.

"When?"

Martin threw another stick on the fire.

"I'll let you know. When you come back with more supplies."

*

I'd never been so glad to be back on the street, running for the cover of light. I stopped to catch my breath against a lamppost. I noticed it was the same one I'd climbed as a kid. The one with a bike tyre snagged half way up on a little wooden box. Someone told me it'd feel nice to stick my fingers in the socket. So I did.

I was electrified.

Now, was my brother's mission the answer to my 'more to life' question? It felt like more.

Rock solid.

I had more awareness of my heart banging. Moths cracking their heads on the Perspex covers of the street lamp above. Someone snoring in the bungalow. The breath of the wind rattling the leaves of a bay tree in the paved front garden. I could taste my insides. Blood in my throat as my chest heaved.

This was definitely more.

But, it wasn't the more I wanted. I wanted something to explain what it was I sensed beneath the surface tension on which we skated, like bugs on a pond. More to quench my thirst. Cool my head. More to turn the poison in my salty veins into medicine.

I closed my eyes and listened for the sea. In the stupor of the summer's warmth, she lay. Sober. Crystal clear. Cold enough to quell our fire. Soak our parched land. To smash our temples down.

The wind picked up. Just a little blast into my face. I could smell the wet chalk and seaweed. The mulchy muscle beds and the mud sand. I could hear the tiny wavelets rushing as she turned. She was definitely coming. Pushed by a bigger force. She was moving. Bringing the answer to me.

I knew then, without doubt, there'd be a price for my knowing this - this more.

And it was weighty.

Let's Submerge

The sun was always welcome. It meant I'd made it through another tormented night. It shone through the curtain rags and hit my bed in a large block of comforting light. Warm and urging. Get up! Get out! Do something! It was still summer. Just. Maybe I should forget about Martin. Treat myself, like the inmates on death row. A last taste of something good.

Singe was at work at the airport, washing planes and Bill was still sweating it out down the pit.

I knew I had to go and say goodbye to my oldest friend.

The beach.

The shifting buffer between us.

Wet and dry.

This was my old life at its best. The summer holidays were heaven. No school. No stiff uniforms. No rules. No changing for sports, showing flea- bitten legs. No showers in front of Mister Morgan, standing with his hands down his shorts, warming his frozen fingers on his bollocks. Liberty. At eight o'clock we'd lay in bed listening to the fog horn groaning. It was the signal telling us it was going to be hot. Grab a worn out towel from the line in the garden. Out of the house in just cut-downs. Better for bombing off the prom in. Towel rolled and wrapped around our necks. No shoes. No lunch. No money. At the corner of Prestwell, we'd meet. Joe, Booton, Frank. All dressed the same.

Gathered, we'd start the walk along Dumpton Lane. Through the Blackberry place, barefoot across the glass-flecked gravel, then down the hill past the really posh houses to the beach. Leave the scrumping for the way back. We just needed to get down there and secure our spot behind the wooden chalets, on the concrete apron under the crumbling cliff.

I laid my towel down and looked around. Through the fading red valerian and dandelion weeds growing from the cracks, I could see the new generation of kids from the estate were camped a little way off. They knew me from the street and saw me as part of their clan. Accepted me as a bigger dog.

"Jumping off?" One of the Sanders chavvies asked me. I didn't know which one he was, there were about eight of them, and the younger ones, other than Frank, all looked the same to me.

"Might do."

They were stoked. I was an ace bomber. I could do suicides dives and all manner of inventive bombs. Like the bigger kids who'd taught me, this lot would keep the tradition going.

"What time's the tide?"

"About another hour yet."

"We'll shout ya."

"Sure."

I lay my head back down and shut my eyes. Their chatter blended with the rolling sea and the gull laughter. The warm sun cooked my back. I was still brown, even though my leather jacket, my second skin, had been peeled off less and less as I'd hit fifteen. Kiddy days at the beach had dwindled. Sure, I came to the beach, mainly at night, to fuck someone, or burn something. But this, I hadn't done for a long time. Jumping off the prom was still a buzz, even if I was jumping with kids.

I opened one eye as I heard a familiar crack. Towel fights whipping big welts on their skinny thighs. The dominant ones would get to take the advertising board up for the old git in the kiosk and get a free ice lolly. The kiosk of dreams. That little concrete box held such fascination for us, until we managed to smash the door in one night. Then, the booty of ice creams and sweets made us puke. Most of them ended up tossed over the railway bridge.

I closed my eye and turned away. I was getting hungry. The sea air always made me hungry. Back then Mum would turn up after twelve, dragging her trolley. Out would come the boiled eggs and salad cream sandwiches. Or corned beef and brown sauce. We'd smash the eggs on our heads to crack the shells, peel them with nimble fingers and chomp away. Bite of egg. Bite of salad cream sandwich. Slug of orange squash from the big plastic container, frozen overnight.

Sickly sweet, but cold. Thirst quenching in the midday sun. We were always swigging the juice, as we couldn't wait for the cups to come out of the trolley. Mum would get annoyed and try to sit us down to eat properly. No chance. We wanted to get our space back, the best spot claimed by our ragged towel, before the others could steal it.

Mum would stay for a while, have a cup of tea from her flask, or sometimes from Auntie Joy who could afford a chalet. Though she never seemed to enjoy that cup. She had to be asked about ten times before she'd accept. Sipping her tea from a little china cup on the beach made her feel what she was, poor.

I can remember the one summer that we had our own chalet. She was so chuffed. Boiling kettles and making teas for everyone. Even people she didn't know, people who'd just stopped for a chat. In her little hut by the beach, she could forget that she came from Prestwell for a while, and slip back into the cosy, middle-class dream she had before meeting my dad.

One season it lasted, then Mum went back to dangling her legs over the promenade and dishing out boiled eggs and salad cream sandwiches, while we spent all day exploring, crabbing, building defenses against the incoming tide. Climbing cliffs, and best of all, jumping off the promenade at high tide.

Defying the worried adults and taking our lives in our hands, we'd run full pelt to the edge of the prom and fling ourselves, twisting and spinning out over the concrete steps, into the sea.

The sea had gasped and turned and now came with some force over the seaweed. Washing away sand boats and castles, delighting the waiting kids. It would soon be high tide.

The youngsters rounded up and headed for the corner of the prom, where the water was deepest. I was forgotten as they lined up, backs against the cliff, ready to charge. Waiting for the wave that would guarantee some depth.

Bemused holidaymakers had stopped to see what the show was. I slipped in, at the end of the line, as the cliff bent around the corner, out of sight from the main body of jumpers. I stood with the hangers-on. They were the youngest, this season's novices. They were pulled forward by the enthusiasm of the jumpers and pushed back by the six-foot drop over the edge of the promenade into the sea.

I knew the thrill of the first jump. Heart in mouth, guts fluttering.

Walking back and forth from the concrete lip above the seaweed-covered steps. Wondering if you could make it and land on the sandy bottom. Pushed and pulled, pushed and pulled. Like the sea itself. Then the tipping point. The 'fuck it factor' kicked in. A deep breath to subdue your insides and you were gone. Feet pounding rough concrete, ear dulled to the urging around you. The terrifying edge came, offering you the horizon of the spreading sea. Sparkling oblivion. And now it was too late to stop. If you faltered here, like some had, the jagged steps and hospital awaited. But in the end, you didn't jump, you just kept running. Peddling soft air. Then the exhilaration of falling.

Budoosh!

Cool salt water hugging as you hit. Stealing your captured breath. Feet and sometimes arse hitting sand below, and then the silence of submersion.

For just a moment.

A frantic push and the explosion upwards, to surface and sharp breaths. Cheering and the welcoming grunts of brothers and sisters.

You had done it. You were in.

I waited for a while. Not sure I could be bothered to jump. Not sure that I wanted to put myself into her. The slapping of bodies against waves and the fizz of the spray hitting concrete lured me. These youngsters were good. It took me years 'till I hit the wall with my splash. The wet ones approached me. Doffing their lank, sun bleached forelocks.

"Jimbo, do a suey!"

"Nah, do a peg-leg!"

I sucked a breath and ran. Nothing in my mind. Just the misty horizon. I didn't want to take my eye off the bitch in case she bit me. At the edge I dived. The punch through and the glide were intoxicating, but all too brief a high. Up and shaking the thump out of my hair on the surface in just a second or two. I wanted to glide underwater like I had in my dreams. Like Superman, cutting through the waves like a nuclear sub.

I swam to the steps.

The youngsters pushed their status by jumping over me. Bombing me. Their small depth charge explosions, surrounded me, spraying white froth. I laughed and pulled them up onto the steps, away from the tide run. Then boosted them up onto the prom for another go.

An unmistakable voice cut through the crowd as I rolled myself up onto the concrete wave wall.

"Long time no see!"

It wasn't someone that I had to clock to recognise. Her lisping loudness was enough. It was Uggy.

I'd first met her on the beach, when I saved her blushes by returning her swimming top, ripped off by a playful cousin. Her first words as she covered her ten-year-old tits were "Friend for life." She'd been right so far. I'd seen her every summer since.

Her mum and dad always had a chalet. They ran a pub in London. Ron was as gobby as his daughter. He used to call us lot the Broadgate mafia. We liked him. He was alright. He'd jokingly tell us to 'piss off', away from his chalet, but then let his daughter bring us up to their house for tea.

Uggy put her arms around me and planted a big wet kiss on my cheek. Her warm tits squashed against me. She wanted everyone to know I was hers. She had a bad habit of invading personal space. Caught off guard I didn't immediately notice someone hanging back behind the prom jumpers.

She had a friend with her.

Uggy took me by the hand and dragged me through the crowd of little scroats to meet her.

"This is Julie. You remember? She came down with me about three years ago. From London."

I must have looked blank.

"We played about on the escalators in Tesco."

Yeah, I remembered Julie. Long brown hair, skinny, freckled face. Uggy, being a good friend, tried to match us up. Not interested then. But shit, I was interested now!

She looked at me shyly and said hello. Our eyes were drawn and repelled like magnets. I started to feel uncomfortable. Then embarrassed by the discomfort. I turned away and looked at the sea.

"You jumping off?"

"Not with this skinny top on." Uggy laughed. "Don't want to flash the world."

"Hasn't stopped you before."

She laughed again, like a drain, adjusting her bikini, wrestling to contain her massive tits. I snuck a glance at Julie. She'd turned her head like a cat, giving me permission to behold her. She was wearing a white blouse tied over her belly. Camouflage culottes and white roman sandals. Her hair was punky, cropped short, the fringe straight and dyed blonde. Her high cheek bones made prominent by her large mouth and slightly protruding chin. Her lips were painted the bright red of plastic apples.

She felt me looking and turned her eyes on me. Deep. Aquamarine. Twinkling with something exotic. Something switched on. I never really looked into people's eyes. They always burnt me. But hers didn't.

They submerged me.

I was glad the moment was broken by a jumper, wanting me to do a suicide dive for the crowd. I turned and ran. I needed to. At the edge I remembered to dive. Arms out wide, body flat, in the suicide position. I held and held, then inches from the stinging surface, I curled forward, and smashed into the waves with all my might.

When I surfaced, the youngsters were cheering. Uggy was laughing her snorting, horse laugh. And Julie, she just stood, a foot back, watching. Smiling ever-so-slightly. Trying to be unimpressed. A thrill shot through me, making my legs spasm under water. Good job it was underwater. I would have looked a right spazz.

Uggy shouted at me from the Prom. "Wanna go out tonight?" I nodded. "Meet at mine. At seven."

I tried to act cool, slowly treading water.

"Might do. Meant to be going out with Singe."

Uggy's face dropped, then bounced back.

"Bring him too."

I turned and started to crawl. Head down, arms pumping, out into the tide run. Out, until the current had taken me away from the shore. Into cold dark water. The depth that scared me. The quiet of the sea out there dimmed even the screaming voices of the jumpers on the prom. I shut my eyes and tried not to panic. If the sea wanted me, here I was, presented.

Helpless.

My screwed-up eyes stung with salt. My heart stuttered.

I held my breath and waited.

A lone fulmar dived down to check me out and wheeled away.

That was it.

Nothing.

A massive smile thrilled through me as I watched Uggy and her friend leaving. Julie made me want to slap the water and scream.

Now she was definitely, definitely more.

A perfect pebble on a beach of bricks.

No Fun

Home and a quick bath. Three hours to kill. Dad was out, gone to see a man about a dog or something. I knew that was code for keep your nose out. Mum made me egg and chips. It was a bit early for tea and she was all smiles. I rooted around in the cupboard under the stairs.

"Seen my jeans?"

"Which ones?"

"The clean ones."

"You're going out?"

"Yeah, with Uggy."

"And her friend?"

I took the plate of egg and chips and walked upstairs. She followed.

"She called me. On the telephone."

"What did she want?" Disinterestedly.

Mum smiled, brightly. She didn't do that often. But where romance was concerned, she'd do a back-flip. Head-over-heels.

"I think her friend likes you." Sing-song. Theatrical.

"Yeah." Piss off. Gross. Keep your nose out. "I'm going out with Bill and Singe."

I shut myself in the bedroom. Smiling. Dunking a golden brown chip into the egg yolk. Fucking hell. I didn't want my mum involved.

Half dressed. Clean pants and socks. Still can't find my jeans. I hear my mum on the stairs. Whispering. Pissy and Nightmare are watching telly in the front room. She's not talking to them. She's on the 'phone. I catch the whisper.

"...and he's had a bath, he must like her."

A snorting guffaw at the other end of the line can only mean she's talking to one person.

Mum puts the 'phone down and sneaks back into the front room, thinking I've not heard her. I want to shout at her, but she's doing me a favour. At least that little bit of doubt is cleared up. She knows I like her. I've had a bath! Being the dirty scummer that I am, I never bath and wash my cock for just anyone!

Thanks Mum.

Now what? Sit twiddling for two hours. In the back garden the cherry tree needs climbing. I hang off a low branch like a chimp. No fun.

No gun. Can't go shooting.

Then I remember. Spiney Collins tried to sell me an airgun last week. He might lend it to me so I can test it out.

"Where are you going?" Mum called out. Slight panic.

"To see someone. About a dog."

"What about going out?"

I walked. Up the street. It was the usual mix of kids on bikes. Some lounging over their cow-horn handlebars, spitting for England. Others wheeled around in tighter and tighter circles, chasing their own arses. Girls slapped boys. Boys slapped back and chased. One of the Houghtons was throwing a house brick against his front wall. It was breaking piece by piece. Orange dust falling onto a pile of already broken bricks.

Spiney's house was at the top end of the Ave. I knew he'd be in. He never went far. His wheelchair was crap. Just about got him to the youth club and back. We used to take him down there, but he talked so much shite we left the job to the McGanns, his next door neighbours. Patrick was the worst. An accident already happened. One night, he caught up with us, pushing Spiney. At the top of the big hill past the cemetery, he took over and jumped onto the back of his chair. Spiney was shouting, trying to put the worn-out brakes on. We watched, laughing, thinking he was just giving Spiney a thrill ride.

A laugh.

But half way down and they were not stopping. Nothing could stop them. Just before the junction at the bottom, with Spiney pleading for his life, McGann bailed. Tumbled over and over, ripping and shredding knees and trousers.

Spiney travelled on, screaming. Across the road, until his trembling front wheels smacked the kerb and sent him flying like a rag doll over the pavement into a garden wall.

The wheelchair span over him into an ornamental cherry tree.

What a bastard McGann was.

We ran down the hill. Our laughter fading as we pushed past the howling twat McGann to inspect Spiney. He was okay. Couldn't have broke his back. Didn't have much of one anyway. I jumped over the wall and got his chair. One of the footplates was gone forever. We dragged him up and heaved him back into it.

"You okay?"

"Yeah, it's just my piss bag leaking." We took him home to change his trousers and got him to the youth club. This time, without McGann riding shotgun.

I knocked on Spiney's front door. His dad, some mad paddy bastard, shouted out. "Trevor's round the back."

I went through the concrete alley between the houses and found Spiney taking pot shots at some tin cans about twenty yards down the garden, as far as the concrete path would carry his wheelchair.

"Jimmy! What ya doing?"

"Just came to see if I could borrow your gun?"

"This one? I'm shooting with it."

"I can see that you spastic."

"I'm not a spastic. I'm a spine-a-biff."

"Yeah. Sorry. Keep forgetting."

I remembered how he told me a giant crab had pinched him in the back, when I first saw his hole. I believed him. Took a lot of explaining from Mum 'till I got the truth. I liked the giant crab story better.

"Can I borrow it? Just for an hour."

"Where ya going?"

"Only up the alley."

"I'll come with ya."

I didn't like pushing him. I wouldn't be able to concentrate on spotting the birds. Too distracted trying to keep his muppet legs from getting caught in the wheels over the rough ground.

"Can I just borrow it, to see if it's got any power. Then I might buy it."

"Where's yours?"

I went to answer, then thought about the psycho in the woods.

"Broken."

"You got any pellets?"

"Nope."

Spiney smiled and I got pushing.

The alley was quiet. A few blackbirds and sparrows hopping about in the ivy. Spiney wanted to shoot everything on our safari. He wanted a trophy to take back. Luckily, for the dunnock he took aim at, he was a shit shot and the gun was as weak as piss.

I managed to wrestle it from him, eventually. I knew how I could kill some time. Using the back pegs on the chair to stand on, I looked over the wall into the posh gardens.

"What ya doing?"

"There's a woman, bending over."

I took aim. Spiney started to push frantically at the wheels.

"Nah. Jimmy. Don't. I can't run." The chair spun in a muddy rut as I fired. Sending the pellet high of the arse target. The women turned sharply. I wasn't sure if she'd seen me. I ducked down. Reloaded. Laughing. Hardly able to insert the pellet into the breech.

Spiney grabbed the gun. "Fuck off! You'll just leave me and I'll get done for it."

I yanked it back. "You couldn't reach over the wall to shoot her fat arse."

"Don't do it! I'll still get done."

I stood up on the chair to fire. Her arse was facing full on as she bent down to weed. Spiney pushed down with both hands and rocked back, tipping the chair. I ended up on the floor. Spiney pissed himself laughing.

I joined in. Then shot him through the leather back panel of his chair.

He fell forward, feigning injury. Hooting and hollering. The pissy pellet wasn't strong enough to give him more than rubber band flick. Then I wondered if I'd shot him in his back hole. His crab attack.

"You alright mate?" He nodded and took the gun from me. I knew I'd have to let him have one back. I started to run. Three steps and twat! A pellet smacked me right in the neck.

"You deserved that, Jimmy. All square. Evens?"

I was about to tip him into a puddle when a pellet ripped past me and thudded into Spiney. He dropped the rifle, holding his wounded arm, yelping like a crab had his finger. I looked round.

Johnny Oldman.

He reloaded and was about to shoot Spiney again.

I stepped into his firing line.

"Fuck off Oldman."

"He shot you!"

"Yeah and I shot him. Evens."

"Yeah, but you can't let a spacka shoot you and get away wiv it." He tried to side step. Spiney grabbed my jacket and pulled me to him, hiding his head.

"You've already shot me once, you cunt."

Oldman wouldn't be called a cunt by a spacka. His mean eyes narrowed. He was going to shoot Spiney, even if it went through me first.

The shot missed my thigh and pinged off the rim of the wheelchair.

Too much. Too far.

I pulled free of Spiney and ran at him.

He brought the barrel up shut and ready to fire just as my fist landed on his jawbone. He looked at me, spitting blood. He knew if he raised the gun I would batter him.

"He's a fucking spacka!"

"So are you! Prick!"

Oldman thought twice. He always did. Coward. Then turned and walked. Half way up the alley, he shouted. "I bet the Old Bill would like to find your brother. Round the woods!"

I grabbed Spiney's gun and fired a shot in his direction.

"Got a spacka gun too!" Oldman taunted as he disappeared into the street.

Spiney went to take his gun back, then presented it to me. "You can have it." I suppose I deserved it. I had protected him.

He stuck his hand out. "Ten quid."

I dropped the gun in his lap and walked, leaving his cack chair floundering in the mud.

"What's he on about ya brother for? Jimmy! Don't leave me here. You can have the gun!"

Someone would get him home. They always did.

I had other things on my mind.

Fucking Oldman. He'd brought it all back. One word to the Old Bill and... my fingerprints were all over that grenade. My gun.

The Robbery.

I walked down the street looking for him. Smashing his face in would be a good waste of time. He was nowhere. Bolted to a rat hole.

I stopped outside his house. If I knocked the rest of them might wanna know why. The sneaky bastard ferret boy must have seen Martin when he'd been shooting round the woods.

Fuck him. He wouldn't grass. Even he wasn't that low?

Spiney's older sister came out of their house, two doors down, chewing on her necklace chain. "Seen Trevor?"

"Yeah, he's up the alley."

"Wanna come and get him?"

Naughty smile. Tight black t-shirt and no bra. Low cut. Like a gymnast. We'd fumbled before. Now she wants to go tumbling with me.

I smile back as I remembered. "Nah. Can't. I'm going out."

"Who wiv?"

"Fishing."

Her face drops. She can't think of a follow up. So she walks, deliberately wiggling her tight little arse in her jeans. She looks back at me flirtatiously. "You're no fun anymore."

Seriously?

Since when has killing time meant to be fun?

(sing if you're) Glad To Be Gay

I walked in on an unexpected scene. My dad was home, sitting in his armchair. Sober. Fucking miracles. My mum was in the cupboard under the stairs, rooting through a large pile of rags. Uggy and Julie sat on the sofa, drinking mugs of tea.

Julie was perched on the arm, legs crossed. She wore a mini-kilt over white tights and tiny bow-topped pumps. Both her and Uggy were done up, ready to go out. Pissy and Nightmare lay on the floor, eating bags of penny sweets. Uggy held one up for me. "Got you some too."

I stared at the bag of sweets, trying not to look at Julie.

"You want them or not?" Uggy waggled the bag at me.

"What you doing here?"

Mum held up an old dress. "How about this?"

"Julie likes fifties clothes. Your mum was trying to find her some."

Julie looked at the crimplene sixties dress and shook her head politely. Mum dove back down into the pile. I must have looked like a right pillock. Standing there, muddy jeans on, muddy boots. Stupid, time-killed expression on my face.

Mum pulled up another dress. Going into overdrive to please her audience. "That's late fifties, ummm, no, more sixties, do you think?"

"Nineteen sixty two. You wore that when Jimmy was born."

Dad was always precise with things like that. Couldn't tell you what he was doing yesterday, but remembered details from decades ago.

"Mum! She doesn't want to see your rags."

"If someone modelled it, it'd look fine."

"You should. Go on Jimmy. Try it on." Uggy smiled, fake pleadingly.

Julie's porcelain face grew a little rosy. Her eyes watched from some great depth within her. They wanted me to.

I peeled off my t-shirt and snatched the dress from Mum. Without undoing the zip, I squeezed it over the top of my head and pulled it down over my jeans. It was quite a good fit.

Uggy snorted, "Looks good on you. I dare you to wear it out tonight."

"We could make him up." Mum suggested rapidly. "Like Danny La Rue."

Dad looked up from his book, which he was reading while watching the TV and listing to us. "Don't go out round here dressed like that, you'll get your head kicked in."

"Go on. Go on." Uggy urged. "Men wear dresses in London all the time."

Julie smiled. Admiring.

"If it's good enough for Captain Sensible, it's good enough for me." I was wearing it. I could dress up stupidly. I could be a tranny if I wanted to. It was punk. "No make-up, though."

Fuck Danny La Rue!

I put my leather on over the top and grabbed the door handle. It was great cover.

"Bloody mental," Dad chirped as the girls got up to leave.

"I dressed like a man once, for one of my stage shows."

Mum was off. When she'd been a show girl, blah blah, dancing on stage and how she nearly got engaged to Ray Allen. Some ventriloquist bloke on TV, with a pissed puppet called Lord Charles.

It really was time to go. Julie was too polite to get up and leave, so Uggy grabbed her gently by the arm and showed her to the door. I was almost outside when I realised I had no money. I pushed back past them in the doorway, squeezing close to Julie. She looked away, like it never happened. Like we never touched. But she was hot and I was starting to catch fire.

"Mum, can I borrow a couple of quid?" I whispered out of Dad's earshot. She went into the kitchen and got her purse from her hiding place, in the bottom of the washing basket. The stage was set for me, but she wanted to be there. Just one dance, a supporting act at least.

"She's pretty, isn't she?" Her shoulders bounced enthusiastically, as she tried to contain her glee.

I couldn't answer.

She shoved two quid into my hand.

"Don't get drunk." She meant 'don't do anything to put that girl off'. I gave her a peck on the forehead. She had nothing to be worried about. I'd put on a performance she'd be proud of.

Dad looked up from his TV-book-trance.

"And don't go doing nothing stupid. You hear?"

I hear. But sorry Dad, doing stupid is me.

New Rose

The Artillery was quiet. It was Thursday. We headed straight downstairs to our bar. A couple of the usual crew looked our way and laughed at the dress, then turned away. It was only me. At least I wasn't on fire or some other stupid shit. Uggy was younger than all of us, but she got served, no problem. Probably the giant tits and quick mouth that did it. She'd worked in her dad's pub, so was completely at home. She was fifteen. I downed the first pint quickly, waiting for Singe, as usual. But now the wait seemed even more unsettling. I had Julie standing before me. Uggy wanted us to talk. But I was struck dumb. Julie's presence kept me staring at the floor or into my pint, anywhere but those blue, bottomless pools. Thankfully, Uggy chatted for both of us, stories from the beach, when we were kids.

I noticed a friend. Ruth. She was half-caste. Indian or something. Or adopted. She was with her white mum and dad. I caught her eyes and she quickly looked away. Panic. What the fuck was she doing in the pub with her mum and dad? She didn't want to see me, for sure.

Mad Mick came down. Got a pint.

"Nice dress."

"I thank you."

I gulped down my drink. Ordered another. Offered Julie and Uggy one. They still had their first. Vodka and tonic and a gin and tonic. Vodka and tonic. All the girls I knew drank Bacardi and coke or cider. She was high class alright.

Why would she fancy me?

Next, some songs on the juke box. Uggy and Julie agreed on Bowie. They left me one credit.

There was only one song.

New Rose by The Damned.

I mouthed the opening line, lifting my magnetised eyes from the floor to meet hers.

"Is she really going out with him?"

She smiled coyly.

I had a chance.

"I've got a feeling inside of me... kinda strange like a stormy sea..."

But how to approach?

Singe and Bill arrived with perfect timing. Bill would chat to Julie. Singe would chat with Uggy. I could just drink and observe. Work my way into it.

Cautiously.

Before the end of the song my trousers had come off. I wound them round and round through the air and let them fly. They disappeared into the pub froth.

I felt the surge of alcohol, hormones and my unease pushing me. My jaw tightened. My eyes widened. I wanted to rush up to Julie and squeeze her. Gurn her. Instead I took my y-fronts off and swung them around my head. They flew from my pointed finger and landed over Mad Mick's pint. He thought it was funny, put them on his head and joined me on the dance floor.

The record changed. Someone else's shit. Some Led Zep song.

Mood killer.

I took the chance to go upstairs for a piss. As I walked away, I caught a sneaky of Julie.

She was safe. Being interrogated by Bill.

I slashed, thinking. I bet Bill would come up to me soon and tell me what I already knew about Julie. She was alright. Class. Bit posh. Shy? From London. Gorgeous. I shook my drips and wanted to get back on with my courtship dance. As I walked downstairs, she was still talking to Bill. I needed to pick up where I left off. I needed a run up.

Ruth and her mum were heading up the stairs. I grabbed hold of the beam above me and swung my legs out. They wrapped around her mum's neck. The dress rode up around my waist as I pulled her head into my naked crotch.

Releasing her from the nude headlock, I jumped down and introduced myself. "You must be Ruth's mum."

Stunned silence.

Ruth's mouth could have swallowed her entire family. Her dad looked me up and down. "Alright. I'm Jim. Ruth's friend." I shook his hand and then leapt over the banister, did a forward roll and stood up directly in front of Julie.

Bill and Singe cracked up. Uggy deafened all within a six-foot radius with her gob.

"What do ya think of my cock?" I said insanely.

Julie smiled coolly.

"Couldn't see it. The post was in the way."

Shit! I was going to marry her.

Bill bundled us away to the next pub before we got thrown out. I made them go into The Lifeboat. A posh yachtie's pub above the harbour. Uggy and Bill got the drinks in while I went into the bogs with Singe. He was out of drugs for once. But I didn't need 'em. I was already buzzing.

"I've got some news," he said sheepishly. Staring at my cock as I pissed.

"What. You're a Homo?"

"Yeah. And I'm going into the Airforce."

"You're fucking kidding?"

"Nope. I'm a queerboy."

I looked at my cock in disbelief.

"You're going in the Airforce?"

"I've signed up. Weapons technician."

"Yeah. Nice one. Believe that mate."

"Nah. Honest. I've got the final induction in three week's time. Then I'm in."

"What!?!"

"I can get a trade. There's fuck all around here. I'm not washing planes all my life!"

The last drips fell into the urinal.

Singe zipped up and shrugged his shoulders. It was done. No more, no less. He walked out, just like that, leaving me to stare at my angry face in the mirror. All the madness, the chaos, had just lost its pointlessness.

Elvis had left the building.

Fucking traitor.

I smashed my head into the mirror. It cracked but still clung to the wall. Shattered.

Bleeding, I went back into the bar. Singe had mooched-off to a table near the cold fireplace, on his own. We joined him. Bill immediately went into one.

"Jimmy, what have you done now?"

I stared Singe down.

Bill guessed. "Singe is joining the Airforce." He announced.

Uggy congratulated him. "I like a man in uniform."

I looked at his puppy face. His eyes watering.

How could I be mad at him?

Easily.

I looked at Julie. She didn't turn away. Instead she passed a tissue to Uggy under the table. For my face.

Shit. I'm such a wanker.

The landlord approached the table and told us quietly to leave.

Outside, Singe switched back on and tanked a car. It was half-hearted. Fake. The girls pulled us down the street to the seafront. At the fight pub, I stopped.

"In here."

"No..."

Bill was too late.

I grabbed Julie and took her into the main bar. Uggy and Singe followed. Rums all round. With blackcurrant to hide its vile taste.

Feeding on the bad vibes from the slags and the wankers all around, I jumped up onto a table and started dancing in my dress and Doc Martens to some camp disco song. I saw Bill's face go from annoyed to scared. Oily Harry and a couple of the Rent-a-Riot dicks were scowling at me from the end of the bar.

I really didn't give a shit. Brother or no brother. I grabbed my crotch and ground it round and round in the direction of Harry's fucked-off face.

I spotted the fire extinguisher and made a move. Bill pulled me backwards and we both fell onto a table of dead glasses. They toppled and smashed with a lovely cascading sound. Like a glass waterfall. The disco song banged on for a couple more seconds. Then, as I stood up, it went very quiet.

The barman, who was out of sight in the saloon, stepped back into the public bar.

"Who done that?"

All eyes on me. Including Julie's.

I stood up straight and went for broke, yelling in my best Kirk Douglas bum-chinned voice. "I'm Spartacus!"

Singe redeemed himself immediately, hollering "No. I'm Spartacus."

Bill muttered some curse about dying under his breath. The Rent-a-Riot lot stared stupidly, trying to get their heads around the guy in the dress taunting them. Oily Harry was a bit quicker and picked up a bottle. This was still his empire and his Rome.

A roar came from the direction of the toilets.

"No! I'm Spartacus!"

Martin, holding an empty glass stepped up from behind, and joined me and Singe. The Rent-a-Riot dicks dropped their doggy pack bristle and smoothed down their hackles. Harry thought about it. Flipping the bottle over and over in his hand.

Martin deliberately let his glass slip onto the floor.

Statement.

It fell into the river of overflowing shards with a deadening crunch. I liked the way the sound was killed. Like a pinging cymbal pinched between chubby fingers. An odd distraction to have at a gunfight. I always did at moments of tension or crisis. I could remember the smell of the copper's aftershave who took my dad away after the big fight with my mum.

It was Old Spice.

Harry planted his bottle on the bar and ordered a pint. He turned to Martin. "I suppose you'll need a fresh glass?"

A peace pint was passed. The glasses swept up and me, happy to have escaped crucifixion, went to see my very own Jean Simmons.

Against all odds, she was still there. Waiting.

Bill, unimpressed by our successful uprising, started moaning. We're gonna get killed. Stabbed. Clubbed. Blah blah. "It didn't end well for Spartacus," he reminded me.

Fuck the power of Rome. I was staying.

So were Uggy and Julie.

I stopped listening to Bill and watched Martin and Harry. They were drinking and talking quietly. Like cell mates. It clicked. Martin was getting info for the robbery. He used to own the arcade. I heard my dad slagging him off when he'd arrived on the estate once, in his old Jaguar. Off to fuck one of his 'whores' up the road. So what was Harry getting from Martin in return? Less aggro? Bill eventually nagged me so persistently that I tuned back in.

"Look just because he's in with Harry, it don't mean you are. We should go."

I looked at Singe. Something was now broken between us. I knew he had to go. Probably had shirts and trousers to iron. I looked at Uggy, she smiled and shrugged her shoulders at me. Neutral. I looked at Julie. She was hard to read. She was happy to stay, to go, to dance the fandango for all I knew.

"Let's have one more," she said without drama.

Result.

Uggy was quick to second the move. She wanted Singe to stay. Before Bill could speak, I got up and moved to the bar to celebrate. I arrived beside Martin and ordered two pints, one gin and one vodka. He stood to attention beside me. I tried to get his eye, but he wasn't for talking. Like he didn't know me.

Bill tapped me on the shoulder. Singe was skulking behind him.

"Don't get us one. We're off."

Bye bye Singe. Bye bye Bill. I nodded. "Later."

Deserters.

I took the two drinks for the girls and came back for the pints. Two for me. Fine. I tried to catch Martin's eye again.

"Still living in the woods?"

"Wearing Mum's clothes?" He spoke looking straight ahead. Was it some sort of homo thing that was weirding him out. Or Oily Harry and the robbery?

"Sit down. I'll speak to you later."

Two pints later and he did. I'd grown ridiculously taut in the meantime. Listening to Uggy, and hanging on Julie's occasional word. I was drinking faster to fill the gaps and getting fuzzier by the minute. My feet were feeling hot, a sure sign my boots were filled. Martin suddenly loomed large at our table and introduced himself. He shook Uggy's hand and kissed Julie on the cheek. Tartily.

Turning it on. Chatting. Rapid bursts of machine gun like questions. Not conversation. Interrogation.

I slumped drunkenly back in my chair unable to keep up with the banter. Uggy was good for a kid. She fired back twice as sharp.

Then I noticed that Martin's foot was touching Julie's under the table.

Playing footsie?

Her eyes smiled at me, unseen by Martin. What kind of a look was that? Did she like it? Was she encouraging him? Was she ignoring it completely and smiling because I was the one she wanted?

Uggy made for a toilet break, taking Julie of course, leaving me with Martin.

I went to ask my questions first, but he shut me up with one statement. "It's still on. Soon." I stammered some shit about why I was wearing a dress in case the weird homo thing was still bugging him. He cut across me.

"Make sure Singe knows he's in. We're gonna need him. Drink up. I'll get you another."

He didn't want to talk about the dress. If he was a bit gay, that would be okay. At least he wouldn't be getting off with my girl.

My brain lurched back to the robbery and Harry as I concentrated on gulping down the last of my pints. The lager seemed slow to disappear. Sludge. Sediment. Earthy.

Spinning.

Uggy came back from the toilets with Julie. She lifted her bag. "We're going."

Martin finished his drink and stood up to leave. With them. With her.

I sat, warm feet melting through my boots and dribbling away into the drains, into the harbour and out to sea.

"Jimmy, you know the way to my house. You can take Julie. Martin and I are going for a walk."

Martin looked pleased, as Uggy put her arm through his and turned him towards the door. For a horrible moment, he was unmoving. But her sheer force of personality and the massive tits, no doubt, tugged him away. Pulled towards the door like a boat on a rope. Slowly at first and then once moving, sliding willingly.

He looked back at me and gave me that look. The one that says 'I'm counting on you, don't fuck up.'

I looked at Julie triumphantly. I was the last man almost standing and I had won the prize. "Shall we go and get out of this dress?"

She smiled kindly at my bravado. Absorbing me as naturally as the sea swallows the dirty estuary.

Take Me I'm Yours

The quickest way to Uggy's was along the seafront and up through the park. It was a still night. Warm. The sea was high and wobbled gently in the dark beneath the promenade. We walked hand in hand, in silence. As we climbed the steps up to the entrance to the park, the air changed. It was charged with crisp autumn cut. Sobering.

The large metal gates to the park were unlocked. The shadows of grass and trees beyond, empty. We joined them in darkness. Our mouths were clamped shut, but our bodies were shouting. Screaming. I could feel excitement in the grip of her slender fingers. My hand was tingling too, but cold and clammy.

I released my grip and put my arm around her shoulders. She looked at me for the first time since we'd been alone. I could just make out the outline of her face in the night's blur. We stopped in unison. She pulled my body to hers, tightly. Our lips found each other and we kissed. Faces melting. I could feel our guts twisting together. Something older than us both, heaved like the sea and came crashing up over. This was something more.

Something inevitable.

But it felt like something I was coming back to. Not something novel.

I knew her. Like an old friend, but in a new body.

It was too fucked up. I broke away, unable to take the intensity. Luckily, I needed a piss. She stood behind me, a few paces back, but even then, I could feel her presence, like she was holding me, helping me stand up.

Uggy's house.

Julie unlocked the door and switched on the hall light.

Empty.

Screaming hard light.

Just us.

I hesitated. Standing like some stupid B-movie vampire on the threshold. "Coming in?" she said sweetly.

I wanted to run. I felt the effects of all my causes piling up inside, like cars crashing on the motorway. I knew without a doubt, that I'd already fucked this up.

But I stepped inside. Knowing I had to let the accident play out.

In the front room, we sat on the leather chesterfield and I let myself fall. Undressing me was easy. I was instantly naked apart from my boots. Her buttons and zips dissolved slowly as we kissed. I could feel my blood surging, the grey wall I'd built for my heart's protection, began to crumble. I tried to hold it, but like a child's sandcastle against the sea, it melted. Overwhelmed by a greater force. The tide, that ride, that urges us forward, to survive, to mate, to live. No matter what dark world we'd created for ourselves, it was always there, shining, pulsing, urging. And in that untouched place, we were at one with it.

She lay back, inviting me to dive in. Twinkling gently like a still, summer's sea. I lay on top and submerged myself, slowly. Irresistibly. She kissed and pulled me down into her. I wanted to pull her back before we went too deep, to share some time on my favourite beach. To visit the place where I once felt...

I wanted to walk amongst the sand dunes. To show her the lizards, skittering across the hot granules. The dragonflies etch-a-sketch flight over the brackish ponds. I wanted us to lay back with eyes shut tight, to listen to the skylarks' blissful babble, and the hunting terns encouraging each other along the shoreline. I wanted time to find the pipit's nest in a warm curl of dry grass, concealing soil-polished eggs. To walk and see the amber eyes of the short-eared owl, glaring as we flushed it from its hiding place.

I kissed and kissed again, but I was held firmly by the present.

I flapped about hopelessly, urging my cock on.

But I knew it was useless.

I surrendered and let myself go under.

"I'm sorry... I'm a bit fucked up... y'know..."

She took my face gently in both hands and whispered "I know." Then she kissed me, softer than before. Kinder. I waited for her to push me away, laughing. But her eyes... I could even see them in the dark. Calm and warm like a windless sunset.

"I'm just too drunk."

"It's okay."

She kissed me again. Stroking my chest. This time, her lips hurt as they snagged on reinforcing wires, my barbed wire defenses rolling back into place along the shoreline.

"Is Uggy bringing Martin back here?"

"No." She turned her slender neck and checked her watch in the half-light seeping from the hall. "She was going to keep him busy for an hour."

That was the plan. They had a plan all along.

"I'd better go before she gets back."

"I don't want you to go."

"Why?"

I felt my groin spasm. Should I try again? I really wanted to leave. To stay. To love her. To destroy myself. To let go. To hold on. I was twisting into some new shape I didn't recognise.

I couldn't stay. I couldn't see Uggy. Grinning. Questioning without asking. Expecting. I dragged myself up and grabbed my dress.

"You can stay the night... if you like."

I left without saying goodbye.

She did call out after me.

Said she'd ring.

Yeah. Like fuck.

I walked up the hill towards Prestwell and stopped on the railway bridge.

So this was it? What I'd been so waiting for?

Something more?

Singe was escaping, but it was too late for me. Nobody gets away with it for long. I'd seen the sea, the true force of nature. It was coming to redress the balance. Starting with me.

I'd finally been caught and strangely, I was glad it was all over.

The dress dropped like a rag from the railway bridge onto the tracks below.

I would walk home with all that I had left - my Doc Martens and my naked defiance.

Fuck it!

Fuck it all!

The Day The World Turned Dayglo

Autumn crawled in. Heavy-limbed, it tilted the Earth and forced summer South. I sat for a couple of days, indoors.

Martin could shoot and steal his own food. I heard he'd broken into the Spar shop. Well, someone had. All the youngsters were talking about it. I didn't really care anymore.

The bedroom boredom leaned on me until I caved.

I had to see Singe one more time before he went.

To say goodbye.

His bike was in one piece outside his house. Freshly polished chrome. Wiped leather and spotless tank. I knocked. The door opened quickly and he chucked me a skid lid.

Surprised. "Where we going?"

Big smile. "Mushrooming."

The sky was the colour of dullness. Thick. Dank-witted. The clouds hung above the land like some retarded dog, waiting to be told. Two days of rain would have soaked into the ground, causing the miles of mycelium to spore. To push forth their slimy fruiting bodies.

It was mushroom season.

We'd first discovered liberty caps by bumping into a mumbling fool outside the off license. He was staring at the lit-up shop window pressing his face against the cold glass. Loving something inside.

We went into the offy and got a few cans. On the way out he stopped us and made a simple pronouncement. "It's magic." That's all he said. But he meant it. We wanted to visit the planet he was on and quickly tracked down our tickets.

A few withered creamy white mushrooms in a newspaper wrap. Infused with hot water in a tea pot and we soon joined the spaceman. Tripping to worlds of our own making. Even Bill joined us, but where we were astronauts, he was ground control. Making sure we always came down safely.

The funniest trip ended in Bill's bedroom. The tea wore off and we all came round together, startled. We knew we'd had an adventure but none of us could remember what had happened. Then I turned out my coat pockets. Piles of dry dirt fell onto Bill's bed. Singe's pockets were filled too. Every available pocket between the three of us, was filled to the top with crumbling nuggets of mud, or as I suddenly recalled, gold.

We were rich only hours ago, sitting in a field on the edge of town, rolling in the finely tilled soil beneath a street lamp, painted gold by the light.

We were hysterical, screeching and whooping, throwing gold dust and solid nuggets into the air. We'd hit the jackpot! We were Klondike rich! Now all we had to do was get the stuff home. We planned to steal a dumper truck from a nearby building site, scoop up our treasure and pile it in my front garden. Then we'd melt it down and make gold bars at out leisure. Fortunately, our mushroomed minds couldn't figure out how to start the dumper, so we gave up and crawled back into our golden field and just took what we could carry.

Singe kicked over the bike and I climbed on. "Is Bill coming?"

"Nah. Going to see his old man," said Singe, tapping the bike into gear and dropping the clutch.

His old man was in jail. For fraud.

The bike's familiar scream echoed between the houses on either side of the street, waking them from their Broadgate slumber. We took off together, like nothing had changed.

But something was moving.

Growing as the earth sipped what fell from the sky, a slow message sent by the sea.

Drip by drip.

It was coming.

The mushroom field was about ten miles away, inland, behind a racecourse. Just one sheep field, about the size of a football pitch. Last year had been a good crop, but by the time we'd been turned onto them, the frost had come and shut the party down. We'd reluctantly bought them instead, at three pounds a hundred. This year, the plan was, we were going to get in early and harvest as many as we could.

Just for us.

We stashed the bike in an old car park, by the abandoned signal station, alongside the railway track. At first glance, we thought we'd arrived too soon. We couldn't see any white caps on the other side of the fence.

Singe stuffed his gloves into his skid lid and looked at me hopefully. "How'd it go with Julie the other night?" I leapt the two strands of barbed wire and mumbled some shit about being too pissed.

"We were steaming alright. Did you fuck her then?"

I stared back, hard. "I don't have to fuck every girl."

"Yeah, but you do!"

"Not this one."

Singe was perplexed. I could feel his eyes breaking into the back of my head as I walked away, across the empty field. Pretending to search.

"Did she give you a blow job?"

"Fuck off! I don't wanna talk about it."

Singe caught me by the shoulder.

"Are you still pissed off with me, about the Airforce?"

"Nah. Why should I be?" I lied.

Singe put on his best serious face. It was pathetic. It made him look like a baby.

"At least you've got a way out. I'm still here. For good."

"I'm sorry Jimmy. I've got to do it. My old man's doing my nut in."

I thought about Julie and what could have been. It was my turn to have the baby face.

"When are you going then?"

"Two weeks."

"Don't 'spose you'll want to rob the arcade with me?"

"I dunno. I've gotta stay out of trouble."

"Can I borrow your bike then?'

Singe's face became see-through. No way was that ever happening.

"You'd wrap it round the first lamppost."

"I suppose I could get little Frank to nick me one."

"Yeah, I can see you and Martin making your getaway, with all that dosh on a Puch Maxi!"

Singe pulled an elfin face as he thrashed an imaginary moped away from the crime scene. "You'll never take me alive, copper!"

I dived on him and pulled him to the ground, playing the cop. "You're under arrest, for driving a shit moped!"

The laughter subsided, sucked into the damp field. Singe looked at me apologetically. "About the Airforce thing. We're still mates. Right?"

I thought about it. Didn't take long. Just a second or two. Why should I be pissed off with him for getting away. Inland. Into the air. This was between me and the sea. It always had been.

"Yeah, course we fucking are."

"I'll steal some bombs for ya."

I remembered the hand grenade. I didn't need his bombs. Or his bike. Just someone to be mad with. To share the sickness with. Singe always made me feel better knowing there was someone else, at least half as sick as I was.

What a way to say goodbye. Picking mushrooms!

The field was on a gentle incline, so we started at the bottom and worked our way up, spaced about four feet apart. By the time we'd made the short climb we'd found zero. The grass was greener, but empty.

"Definitely too early." Singed puffed.

I bent down and eyed the smallest pointed cap, straining to get over the top of a tuft of grass, growing around some sheep shit. Gleefully, I picked the tiniest magic mushroom ever and showed it to Singe.

Behind his foot was another. Bigger this time. And another. "Magic." We both intoned together.

Walking back down the same way as we'd climbed, we picked about a hundred in less than ten minutes. Singe started munching a few.

"I'm not getting on your bike with you tripping."

Singe dropped the rest of his handful into my carrier bag. We did another sweep, this time we were surrounded by mushrooms. Thousands had appeared from the soil. Maybe it was just the psilocybin leeching through our fingers, making us trippy, but they were popping up everywhere.

Our harvesting was rudely interrupted by a Landrover bombing over the field, scattering sheep in all directions. We knew we had to get back over the fence, which we did. Like a couple of gymnasts, vaulting for fun.

"Get out of here now!" The purple-faced farmer ranted. "I'm calling the police."

We knew they couldn't touch us on this side of the fence, even with the shrooms. As long as they weren't dried, we could munch them in front of their faces if we wanted to.

There was no way the fat git could climb the fence, so we rode by, giving him the two fingered salute, and left in a cloud of dust. Thankfully, Singe managed to stop where the dirt track met the main road, as we almost slid under a horsebox steaming towards the jump meeting at the nearby track. Levelled up, we were soon roaring back towards Broadgate with our booty. A thousand or so magics to play with. One last sick trip together before the Airforce made a better maniac out of him.

*

It was a shit trip. Bill got us listening to Pink Floyd and kept going on about the prism on the album cover and how the light was splitting. Singe seemed to shrink and sat at the end of the bed, looking at his tiny hands. I went inward. Bad move.

It's not good inside my head.

Alone, I followed the Yellow Brick Road, through the woods, out the back of Oz into some kind of multi-storey car park filled with all sorts of abandoned causes. I slid down a slippery exit ramp and found myself sitting at the bottom of a concrete road tangle, beneath a huge overpass, on which I could hear the constant roar of all life, earth-bound and interstellar, heading somewhere. Everywhere.

Surrounding me were hundreds of versions of myself, all seemingly lost. We had meaningful conversations until I'd ask them to show me the way out. They'd be struck dumb and run away, looking for their vehicle. Something to carry them to places they belonged. But like me, they were all hopelessly lost and the signposts around us pointed everywhere at once, and all mysteriously led back to where I sat.

Nowhere.

Shivering.

Forever.

For a moment I became aware that I was tripping. I had to do something to get out. I stopped a future version of me, juggling fresh causes of infinite possibility. He held out his hand and said he knew the way out of this hell. I trusted myself and took my own hand. I opened a door inside him and stepped through onto my favourite beach.

The sand was warm and the water crystal. The breeze was cooling and it was the perfect time, just before high tide. I stepped into the water and waited for a wave. A giant tear rolled in from somewhere emotional, across her face. It picked me up and carried me inland, causing such delight that all the birds flew up from the dry fields and played guitar solos on the edge of their feathery wings. Pink Floyd's wet dream flowed from speaker-ears and cascaded across the patterned bedspread of Bill's bed. Stranding me like jetsam on a floral tideline.

I was down.

Singe smiled at me inanely. "Magic?"

I kissed the wall and left. Glad to be back in the boring regularity of the 'real world'.

Fucking mushrooms.

Raw Power

Nothing much happened in the shutdown. Broadgate let out a long, dissatisfied sigh. Another summer over. Things started to dry up and blow away. The kids went back to school. The tourists went back home with their kiss-me-quick hats, crabs and sticks of rock. Birds pissed off south. The nights had an edge that made me zip up my leather. The rain got wetter. The scent of mushroom decay began to seep into my nose. The earth's mouldering sent a signal to the sea, turning its cheerful summer sparkle to mud. The waves got short. Choppy. Agitated. Low pressure was building. Forties. Dogger. Humber. Force five possibly, seven. And rising.

Storm force nine.

I wanted to leave. The swallows were feeding up their young, busying themselves on the telephone wires outside. I was waiting. Jealously. A growing hatred inside. I wanted to be part of the migration. The movement. The tide. The spinning of the earth, the churning of the galaxy, the stretching of the universe. But I was stuck. Feet planted in a chemically farmed field, hemmed in with fences. Like some mutant corn cob.

Singe was getting out. Bill was already gone. I kept thinking about Julie. How I had a chance and fucked it up. I should just go. Somewhere. Anywhere. But I knew I had to stay. To die with everyone else.

Oldman threw a stone up at the swallows, scattering them. "You're brother's living up the flats now. Wiv some fat bird." It was a peace offering. Sharing general knowledge. I let it slide. Nobody was looking for Martin. The MPs hadn't been back and I began to wonder if the robbery was still on. Oldman ran after me as I walked back through the alley. He stopped at a respectable distance.

"Are you doing the job wiv 'im?"

Rooted.

"What?"

"The job. Are you doing it wiv 'im?"

I walked on, stiffly.

"Don't know what you're on about."

He bowled up beside me.

"I think Old Harry's got him up to it. So I've heard."

I jumped the small gate and grabbed him by the scruff.

"Listen, you fucking idiot. Keep your mouth shut!"

He smiled at me. Confirmed. He was doing it.

"I won't say nothing. You know I ain't a grass."

"Who told ya?"

"Fat Georgina, up the flats."

I let him go and walked on. Who else knew? Prestwell had no secrets. Everyone knew everyone's business. Fuck all else to do, but gossip.

"You tell anyone and you're dead."

I knocked on Fat Georgina's door. She answered after I'd been slapping the letterbox for a while. Her face was made harder by wearing her short hair, cropped at the sides. Her fat, tatt-smothered arms were crossed, pushing her tits out over her vest top. To the limits of their stretch marks. She coughed and shouted over the Bob Marley inside.

"Martin. Brother's here."

Martin finally came to the door, in his jeans. Top off. He looked behind me. Like he'd lost something.

"Where's Singe?"

I shrugged my shoulders.

Polishing his boots?

He didn't invite me in. I could smell the sickly odour of hash. He pulled the door almost shut. He was relaxed, in his own psychotic way. Eyelids drooping over glazed eyes. Mouth slightly open. But his six-pack was twitching. Muscles fighting with each other to be on top.

"It's on, tonight. We need Singe's bike. Just in case."

"Tonight!"

Singe's bike? A getaway, for two. But there would be three of us. I got it. He needed the bike for himself. So he could get away. He couldn't afford to get caught. Maybe I would get on the back with him.

Or Singe.

"Meet down by the clock tower. Twenty-two hundred hours. I'll bring the kit we need. Any questions."

I stood dumbly trying to work out when twenty-two hundred hours was.

He prodded me in the chest.

"Questions?"

"How're we gonna carry the coins?"

"Coins? The coins go to the bank. The real money stays in the safe. No income tax. He keeps it all there until he goes to Spain in October, 'cept he's going to be a bit light for this holiday!"

"Are we using the hand grenade?"

Martin's eyes strained open a little wider, setting free a devious smile.

"It's easy. You just stick it to the safe with the tape and pull out the pin."

That was more than enough information for me. I was going to get to pull the pin! I wanted to blow things up. Like in the movies. The cowboys would always use sticks of dynamite. Just enough time on the fuse to dive for cover. The grenade was just as good. In my mind I'd hear the fizzing fuse as I ran from the amusement arcade. Kaboom! Dollar bills would be settling on the burnt shell of the office. Singe and I would be stuffing them into our hats, with urgency. Laughing like tequila-crazed bandidos.

"Twenty-two hundred. Don't be late. Tell Singe to fill his tank up."

The door shut leaving me to walk the long balcony. Alone. But the windows, I'm sure, were stuffed with eyes. Watching.

*

The day soon decayed into evening. The sky was pissed off and low hanging. Fast moving ranks of clouds rolled across the sky. The wind started to rip at the orange and yellow leaves on the cherry tree in the back garden.

It was meatloaf and chips tonight. And tinned tomatoes. My dad had his dinner on a tray in his armchair. We sat on the sofa. On the coffee table were twelve or so slices of Mother's Pride white bread and marg for making butties. My dad was having gammon steak and was smiling. The pineapple always sat on the side of his plate until the end, when he'd give it to the dog.

They both hated it.

Mum seemed happy for a change.

"Did your dad tell you about his job?" I shook my head as I folded the deep brown chips into the bread blanket. "He's got a start on the new sea wall. It's going to take two years to build."

"Eighteen months."

Dad quickly corrected her.

"Yeah, but it might last longer." She said hopefully.

I was glad. Stop them arguing, but really, what a waste of time. Trying to stop the sea.

Mum stood right in front of the TV to get his attention.

"Go on, tell him."

My dad stopped carving his gammon.

"What?"

"About the job. What you've found out."

That was enough. I nervously stuffed the last of my buttie and got up to go. I didn't want to talk to them about 'the job' just in case it was the one I was doing with Martin in about two hours time.

"You tell him. Can't you see I'm eating."

Mum almost danced toward me. "Dad might have got you a job, with him on the sea wall."

"Great."

"You could earn about one hundred and fifty pounds a week." Mum clapped her hands like a wind-up toy at the top of its spring.

"He'd have to work bloody hard though. I'm not carrying him."

Dad dropped a small piece of gammon to the dog.

Celebration or what! I couldn't say anything. I was listening to the wind starting to howl through the alley and the rain pissing onto the window. Wondering how we were going to get down onto the roof of the arcade.

"Good isn't it?"

"Yeah."

I got up and dragged my leather from its lurch.

"You're not going out tonight? There's a storm coming." Dad was giving more gammon to the dog. "Tidal surge as well. They're expecting damage."

Mum sat on the arm of his chair. Beaming. "More work for you then!"

Dad gave her eyes. She moved like the dog did, sidewards back to the sofa.

"I'm just going round Singe's."

I gave the last couple of chips on my plate to the dog. Super-heaven. I patted it on the head, goodbye. I did the same with Pissy and Nightmare on the way out.

Nightmare grabbed my leg and clung on. Crying.

"Don't go Jimbo. Don't go."

Mum had to pull him off. Weird little thing. Like a dog sensing an earthquake. That's why he had nightmares. Sleeping next to me must have been like sleeping on a fault line.

The trill of the 'phone cut through. Mum answered it, sitting on the telephone seat. She bubbled excitedly.

"James. It's for you."

It was the only person I wanted to talk to.

But not here.

Not now.

"I told you I'd call you."

Silence.

I could almost touch her through that velvet quiet.

I couldn't move my limbs.

My lips.

"He's gone all shy!" Mum teased.

I wanted to punch her.

"What's your number?"

I put the 'phone down and headed out.

Dad mumbled. "Don't be out long. I'm taking you down early, to see the foreman."

In the piss-stinking 'phone box round the corner, I pulled the heavy metal door behind me. The wind sucked, playing it like an accordion. Finally it pinched shut and sealed me inside. I put the ten pence in the slot ready and dialled.

I don't think it even rang once before she answered.

"Hello?" Her voice was warm sand, lapped by cool sea. "What are you doing?" she asked politely, like I might be going to have dinner with the Queen.

"Going to see Singe. What you doing?"

"Ringing you."

"What for?"

"Wondered if you wanted to come up this weekend. Mum said you could stay."

"_____"

"Jimmy? You still there?

"_____"

Now her voice cooled. Waves dumping.

"Do you want to come and see me or what?"

I think I must have been silent for a while 'cause the pips went as my ten pence started to run out.

"Yeah. I really..."

Dialling tone.

Drone.

I could wait. Maybe she'd ring me back?

I waited.

Nothing.

A small golden moth flew around the 'phone box light.

Wait.

Just one more minute.

I think she meant it. I could stay at hers. At her parents. I'm sure that's what she said. Parents?

My last ten pence. I rubbed it nervously, trying to split it into two. I put it in the slot and dialled. It rang and rang.

Finally. A slight pause. They didn't want to pick up.

"Hello?"

"Singe... It's on."

Small Change

The rain was starting to get to me by the time I'd walked to Singe's. I wondered if he'd still be up for it. One last blast before he got indoctrinated. Or would he stay on the straight. Keep out of trouble.

All the houses were alight behind curtains. Burning. Yet they sat and watched TV. The storm would have to rip the rooftops off before they noticed they were on fire.

I knocked timidly on Singe's door. His old man answered. Like he'd been waiting, standing behind. He stared down at me, soaking in the rain. He was a big trunk of a man. He swayed gently, controlled. He was drunk. Glass of hard stuff in his hand.

"Alan, it's your MATE."

I was everything he hated, 'the youth of today', ill-disciplined, lazy, destructive, insolent. All the things he'd had bashed out of him by the Army. Things he'd been forced to remove and replace with smartness, external discipline and the amazing ability to tow the line. "Yes sir, no sir, three bags full sir..." I could see how attractive that was right now. As I was about to go and do something I knew to be the stupidest thing I'd ever done in my life. How nice it would be to have someone controlling me. But no sergeant could. No parent. No copper. No judge. No politician. No god. No devil. Not even me.

I had no reason to.

The world had lost any reason and me with it. And somebody expected me to behave?

Singe's dad left me standing in the rain to make his point. I unzipped my leather, made out I was enjoying it.

"You're not clever ya know." His eyes cut, as he tried to look into my soul, but his gaze was easily blunted. There was no soul in me to see, but whatever spirit remained was on lockdown, deep inside, in solitary confinement. For its own protection. Then he smiled at me like he'd remembered something, like he'd won.

"Alan's joining the Airforce next week. Did he tell you?"

I didn't answer.

"And you know the best thing about it?" He raised his glass to toast me, "he'll be away from you lot."

 Singe appeared in the door wearing his crash helmet and gloves and holding a spare. His dad blocked his exit.

"Alan, you're mad if you think you're going out on your bike in this."

"We're only going to Bill's."

"Well, walk then."

Singe pushed past him and chucked me a skid lid. I slapped it on and saluted his dad as he kicked the bike over. Singe pulled away pretty slowly as the front door slammed and his dad's smile faded.

Have another drink. That's what men do. Self-congratulation. Well done, you've got a son, someone to do all the things you couldn't. But when he doesn't turn out to be like you, you can always blame the milkman.

I expected Singe to speed up when he turned the corner and headed down the long road to the town centre. But he just kept at a steady speed.

Crawling speed. Maybe he didn't want to kill himself before he went away.

The wind buffeted us. The rain fell, elongated, like bolts. Maybe it was the storm.

"Speed it up! I'm getting soaked."

Singe slowed the bike to smooth stop.

"Hold on Jimbo." His voice was muffled and distant. I grabbed the back of the seat behind me, expecting a burst of speed. The pull away was lame. Again we settled at about twenty. Not even ramming speed.

"C'mon! Let's go!" I shouted. Singe kept the throttle even. The Old Bill passed slowly in a blue and white. Pulling out from a side street. I got it. He was just making sure we didn't get nicked on the way to the job.

At the cliff top, by the clock tower, we stopped. The place was empty.

The wind was keener. Tripping over the rain to get inland. A builder's bucket tumbled head over heels along the lubricated road.

You never usually notice the sea until you're right on it. But she had grown legs and was rushing all over us. The noise was white. Roaring. Churning beneath the wind. Growling.

I looked to the clock tower. Martin was absent. Across the little public garden was a shelter. Opened to the elements. Behind it seemed like a good place to wait.

I jumped off the bike and motioned for Singe to follow me. But he sat. Engine running. Visor down. A thought flashed through my mind. He was going to leave me. I grabbed his arm.

"Let's wait by the shelter."

He didn't move.

"Out the rain."

Nothing. I flipped up his visor. His eyes were staring at the rain melting into yellow snakes in the beam of his headlamp.

"You tripping?" He waved one hand and wiggled his fingers like he was ruffling the hair of a wind-blown Goddess. He grinned at me stupidly from this other world. I slapped his visor down. "Wait here."

I ran across the streaming road and backed into the rear of the shelter. Martin scared the life out of me, appearing from inside. In his hand, a black rucksack and a length of coiled rope.

"We still doing it?" I shouted stupidly through the gale.

"Yeah. Nobody's around in this shite." Martin looked across at Singe. "What's he doing over there?"

"Keeping the engine running, in case the Old Bill come."

"Let's do it."

Martin walked easily through the blasts coming over the cliff. Head down. I struggled to the railings above the arcade. Salt spray tingling, fixed on my lips by the kiss of the gale. Martin tied the rope and dropped it. It snaked madly. Flexing like it'd been electrocuted. Gloves on. Martin grabbed the rail to vault.

"I know a safer way. By the lift. You can go down the wall. There..."

I pointed out an ornamental wall, about a foot wide that sloped down from the top of the lift. At the bottom it was still about ten feet from the rooftop, but I'd rather hang down and drop than take my chances on the rope.

"Can you get down onto it?"

"Yeah. Easy. I done it before. Getting my ball back." I lied. Anything was better than the rope.

"Okay. You go down. I'll use the rope."

It was easy getting over the railing onto the side of the lift. The wall sloped steeper than I thought. It looked slippery. One advantage was the lift facade cut out most of the wind. The spray swirled quietly round the apex of the wall, caught in the security light.

I climbed onto my belly and began to monkey down. Martin dropped the rucksack onto the roof and lowered himself over the edge. The clattering of the crow bar inside, a muffled tinkle.

At the bottom of the wall I eased myself onto the ledge. Flat against it, I dropped one knee. Left hand down. Grab. Right hand down as my right leg flopped over the ledge. I tensed. Boots scraping down the wall. Then I hung as low as I could and let go.

Thud. Heap. Roll. I was down.

Martin was waiting. He looked like he could have done the rope with me on his back.

Army training. Useful for robberies.

We crossed on the spine, over the glass roof of the outer arcade. Fifteen feet above sea level. The waves were smashing over the prom and fizzing like Alka-Seltzer across the tarmac. I stopped and watched the white brine melting around the folding wood and glass doors of the outer arcade.

"Oi! Get over here." Martin called out from the solid, felted roof of the main arcade. A skylight dropped down into the office. He took the crowbar and levered it open like a tin of pop.

"What about the alarms?"

"Only the doors are alarmed."

He took another neatly folded rope from the rucksack. Tied it to the centre of the crowbar and wedged that across the skylight. A short slide and we dropped onto the cheap carpet of the office.

I burnt my hands and cursed under my breath.

"You don't have to whisper. There's no one here."

Martin kicked open the flimsy adjoining door to the storeroom. Sitting between two shelves filled with office supplies and bits of fruit machines was the safe. About four feet square. Gun metal grey. With a steel handle and combination lock. Exactly like I'd imagined.

Just like the movies.

I picked up a bag of five pence pieces from on top. Must have been about five quid inside. I stuffed them into my jacket pocket and reached out for the others. Martin tossed the grenade to me.

"Concussion grenade. More explosive."

He ripped off some of the thick gaffer tape. I lifted the grenade and held it while he laid a length across one side.

"I'm going to hold down the safety. You pull the pin. You stick it and then we run."

Martin moved my hand, manoeuvering the grenade towards the side of the safe.

"Okay." I hesitated. "Just pull and twist. I've got the safety."

I pulled with a twist. The pin came away with more resistance than expected. I froze.

"Stick it."

"How far?"

"How far what?"

"How far do we run?"

"Until I say so."

I carefully smoothed the tape onto the cool metal of the safe.

Safe wasn't a good word right now.

Martin let the safety bar spring. The grenade hung.

Perfectly.

"Run."

I ran, brain shrieking, through the office, out into the black arcade. Martin dived behind a kiddie's car ride. I kept running. Almost to the outer arcade before it exploded.

I don't know if the blast knocked me down or I just tripped. But as dust and paper and bits of dry wall bounced around me, I looked along the grubby squares of carpet floating beside me and noticed the sea.

I was in it. About four inches deep inside the arcade. Black. Cold. Lapping. The wind outside was pumping at the folding doors. They croaked and shuddered. Bellows sucked by the gale. White spume slugged its way up the outside of the glass and broke off into the air. Twisting under the metal street lamp, it was sucked upward into the rampant sky.

I found Martin in what was left of the storeroom. The walls had blown and lay covering the office. I expected to see him stuffing his bag full of money. Instead, he was trying to force the unmoving safe door with a second crow bar. The side was dented and blackened. But that's all.

Martin saw me dripping behind him.

"Fucking thing didn't blow." He stuck the crowbar into a gap the dent had made in the side of the door.

"Help me lever it." Futile. But I wrapped my wet hands around the bar and tried to help him pull.

The sea showed us how to break things. One wave jumped the prom and rolled over the tarmac, rearing up like a snake to strike. The outer doors caved and sailed across the arcade, smashing glass and metal amusements. Scattering our small denomination.

I ran to the edge of the outer arcade to see the waves hitting the bingo seats, washing even the larger machines around. They floated like untethered barges into one another. The noise was horrific. The scraping of glass and metal and the thunder of the sea and wind jabbing, hooking and slapping with its backhand. The door alarms weaving in and out of the cacophony.

"Come on. Withdraw. Let's get out of here."

Martin pulled me back towards the skylight as another larger wave bulldozed through the arcade, sucking down a section of the glass roof.

I pulled myself up, outside, and saw how close she was. The building shook as the beating intensified. Just beyond the flat roof the sea was unleashing. The spray spat from her salivating lips and arced over us like bullets into the cliff wall. The wind had worked itself into a fevered hysteria and was no longer gusting, but blew with one extended scream.

Martin ran across the roof and grabbed the fitting rope. He'd started climbing by the time I noticed someone sitting on the apex of the outer arcade. Black leather jacket and gloves. Jeans ripped at the knees. Wearing a full-faced crash helmet.

I crawled onto the creaking spine towards him.

Aware of everything and nothing, Singe turned from the show and waved at me. A spaceman about to take a small step for mankind.

He gently pulled off his helmet and stared into the storm. His trippy eyes expanding into the blackness and beyond. Out from our wet little planet into the silence of dry space. The solar wind caressed his hair. Weird static made it stand on end, strands dancing weightlessly. The electrons and protons of dying starlight bounced off him like the agitated bingo balls in the sea beneath. He stood up and held out his hands in the wonder of it all. I called, calmly. Trying to get his attention. I screamed, trying to pull him back to earth.

But he was gone.

Cord cut, he drifted away into the space opening up before him.

The waves took the remaining support from the roof and it collapsed into the churn. Taking Singe with it.

I crawled to the edge of the shaking roof and looked down into the raging water. Singe was laying on his back inside a broken Penny Falls machine. Floating on a barge of copper coins and shards of sharp, wet glass.

His eyes were gone, but his mouth was still here, smiling.

Another large wave tipped the floating arcade machine and Singe was sucked down, chewed with wood and sparks and glass. Smashed and dragged away, so easily. So flimsily.

I lay on the flat roof and tried to fight back the odd calm that filled me.

The wind caught its breath and I heard Singe's bike leaving up on the cliff top. I rolled over to look for my friend. For a sign of life. But now the sea was taking the spoils of its raid away. Flotsam made its way towards the edge of the promenade and dropped off the hard world.

I wondered if he would still be tripping.

A siren sounded. Fire Brigade? Old Bill?

I needed to move.

I grabbed the rope and climbed. Like in my dreams, chased by monsters. If I looked back I knew I would fall and die. But unlike my dreams, my straining arms had to get me to the top. I couldn't let go and scream before I hit the floor, and wake up, safe in bed.

The wind twisted me like an Action Man dolly. I smacked into the cliff. Again and again. The bag of coins in my jacket pocket punching me in the ribs. My fingers weakened.

I reached the top of the rope. Just needed to get over the concrete to the railings. My fingers thrashed at the rail.

Slippery. No grip.

A sense of quiet, an eye in the storm.

Was it really my time to fall?

To give in?

My arm was grabbed and held tight through the railings.

Oldman's face strained through the metal bars. "Grab on Jimbo!"

I managed to get my leg up onto the cliff apron. Oldman pulled on my leather, helping me to stand. I flopped over, onto the floor.

He bent down to me.

Stoked.

"Did ya get anything?"

Old Bill, blue light flashing, came out of the rain. I ducked behind the shelter with Oldman.

Sea-shocked.

I looked along the cliff top. That way, home, the one place I always ran to. One of the Houghtons, his younger brother and a couple of the other youngsters, stood along the cliff, watching the arcade losing its fight with the sea.

It was a night out for them.

They stood cooing and laughing as the waves smashed in.

I took the bag of coins from my pocket and dropped them into Oldman's hand.

"Is that all ya got?"

I felt sick.

Salt. In mouth. Sick.

"Yeah."

"I thought you'd get more."

I started laughing. "More!" My cackling weirded him out. Big time. I held my hands up to the storm, like a mad preacher.

"What 'more' do you want than this?"

He didn't get it. It wasn't a joke. So why should he?

Anyway, he truly belonged to the land.

He turned to join the other kids from Prestwell, watching their future breaking, a worthless arcade, emptied of pennies.

Over his shoulder, laughing spitefully, Oldman got his last word in.

"Oh yeah, yer brother told ya to 'fuck off!'"

Storm The Gates of Heaven

I walked into the Artillery expecting everyone to know. I braced myself. But nothing. The upstairs bar was pretty empty. No-one I knew. I ordered a pint. Then checked to see if I had any money. None. Shit. My brain was all over the place.

"I'll get it." The guy on the stool. Droopy moustache. Stoned-happy. I took the drink and nodded my thanks. "You're Tony's boy, aren't ya?"

Tony. Yeah. Dad. "That's me."

He stuck out his hand. "Rob. I worked with your dad. Good man." I remembered him now. Played cards at my house. Took most of my dad's wages. I got pissed on his whiskey when I was ten.

I didn't shake his hand.

"What you doing out. In the rain?"

I looked at his jeans. Flared. Dry. Shirt, denim, dry.

"Looking for my mate."

He took a drag on his fag and blew the smoke up, away from me. He nodded knowingly. I took the pint and turned away. I recalled my dad telling me how Rob had died.

Drowned in his bath.

I went downstairs without looking back. Leech was speed-freaking with some doper. I'd seen him around. He was a junkie.

A sly, untrustworthy type.

Leech didn't see me. Was he dead? Not yet.

The junkie might as well be.

I sat at a small table under the stairs. Next to Singe. He was smiling. Looking at something neither of us could see. I didn't know what to say to him.

Who would.

Leech tapped me on the shoulder. "Jimmy Jimmy. Wanker. You ok? Want some speed?" He lent closer. "He's got some smack if you like?"

I declined.

"What you doing down here? Fucking dead tonight."

I shivered.

"Wanna come to a party. Bit hippy-dippy, y'know. Hey, you got any of those Erics?"

I shook my head and looked at the empty seat where Singe had been.

"Where's Singey? Has he got anything good?" Leech took four blues from his pocket and gave them to me.

"I'll have some Erics when you get some. Right. Owe me. Party! Address. You know up by the cemetery. Ray's House. The hippy twat. Should be a laugh."

Leech heard the door go and went upstairs. I swigged the blues down. I needed to go to the cemetery. To check something.

*

The cemetery was noisy. The trees were shaking their boned hands in the wind, lamenting. Leaves crunchy underfoot. Dead. The branches creaked like the old boats I'd seen on pirate films. The ones haunted by dead sailors, drowned by the sea.

I sat next to my favourite grave. The speed was kicking in. I talked a while about my arse being wet. The fucking noise of the trees. There was no response. As usual. Nobody there.

I was hoping Singe would pop up and start rattling chains or something daft. If he'd been a ghost he'd definitely do something like that.

But he was just dead.

A memory flooded over the folds of my brain, then receded. I could see him now. Clearly. But in time, like my nan, my grandad, my dad's card hustling friend, Rob, he'd drain away. Fade into black and white like the old soldiers on the TV footage.

A speedy thought flashed. Was Singe in heaven?

I imagined that punishment. Perpetual boredom and all those heavenly bastards with their harps singing 'I told you so.' He'd be trying to set fires and would be forgiven with the same self-righteous breath that blew out his matches.

There was no soul-searching needed. Nothing to reconsider.

He was just dead.

Though there was something of him in the storm ripping at the branches. Something wild and wonderful. Something of him in the sea that took him. Something vital that couldn't be tamed.

Something borrowed that she'd now reclaimed.

Riders on The Storm

I was chewing my teeth down to nothing by the time I found Hippy Ray's. I knocked at the door for ages before Leech let me in. Inside a room, with a beaded curtain for a door, they all sat cross-legged on the floor. Deep in smoke and The Doors. Leech said there was no beer. A bottle of sherry was all he could find. Some party. I swigged some of the sweet shit down. A girl, a fat hippy with her hair in braids, welcomed me into their circle.

One of them, the oldest guy there, said "punks are cool," and pulled a cushion up beside him. They offered me a joint. I took a pull. It was herby sweet. I stared at the rug in the centre of the circle. It seemed to be the main attraction.

I tried hard to look for what it was they were seeing, but images of Julie, the dress, the waves, my dog, the nuggets of gluey sap on our cherry tree, the broken clock on the living room wall, a James Bond car I got for Christmas, the little man I lost from its ejector seat on Boxing Day, a magpie, a crab, a silver spoon with BEA embossed, this and thousands of other useless pictures sped by.

Or was it me moving?

I rushed by like a speeding train. My amphetamine eyes glimpsing my still life through the window.

Without realising, I'd been talking out loud at the same speed.

The older guy applied the brakes.

"Woah, man. Slow down. Take it easy. Life is better when you take it slowly. Savour."

They nodded. Group mentality enhanced by dope. I wanted to be with them. It seemed peaceful there. The Doors sang about us being riders on the storm. I took another toke on the joint and tried to hold the smoke in. To ride with them. The older guy smiled at me expectantly.

"Sometimes you can't do anything but go with the flow."

Leech had stopped jabbering to the fat girl in the kitchen. I could see him lighting up some tin foil. Chasing. The girl held the silver while he sucked the smoke. Nobody but me noticed, as he slipped into the brown quagmire.

All remaining eyes were on me. I must have been talking some shit. A young guy, about my age, an apprentice hippy with curly hair and wearing a denim waistcoat and flares, passed the joint on and nodded slowly at me.

"Nothing to freak about, man. We're all in the same boat." He shook my hand. "I'm Ray. This is my humble abode. What's your name and what's your game?"

"My game? My game? I don't know... I see things sometimes."

"Cool." Cooed the third drip.

"Your name?" spoke Ray.

"Jimmy."

"Jimmy who sees things sometimes. I liked your stream of consciousness. Something cosmic going on."

"I saw the sea and it's coming to swallow us all. But it didn't. Yet. Just my friend, and I thought it was coming for me." Ray reached out and tried to put his arm around me. I pushed it away.

He smiled then and smug-mugged me.

"The age of Aquarius. He's right, it's coming for us all." They nodded together and slowly, one by one, sunk into the tinkling of the piano and the rumbles of thunder. And the carpet. I wanted to believe something at that point. Anything. There was comfort in their group. Their vibe was soft and had no edges. No barbs. I tried hard to melt into it. But the more I pushed, some invisible rubber wall bounced me. I sat on the outside looking in. Just like them. Disconnected, in a group of one.

They were hiders from the storm.

But they were wrong and so was I.

Nothing was coming for us all.

Just for each one of us.

In the kitchen, Leech was slumped into a chair. The fat girl shaking his unconscious body.

Party over.

Television's Over

It was nearly five when I got home. I had to go in and get some stuff. I crept in. The house was silent. Everything off. Unplugged and closed for the night.

Upstairs I could hear my dad snoring. The dog was on the sofa. He looked at me with his guilty eye. I sat next to him and patted his fat body. He licked me once and went back to sleep. I looked at the resting house. It was spooky when it was quiet. Without the telly talking and singing and squawking. Without Pissy and Nightmare fighting. Without the bickering. The cooking. The music. The arguing.

The laughing.

The TV gave us that at least.

I wanted to plug it in, but I knew all that would be on was the dead hiss of the shutdown. Something I couldn't watch anymore. No comfort in the buzzing dots.

The noise had been silenced.

I felt sad. But why? Didn't I want to escape from this? I thought so, once. But this was new. Something more.

They were just trapped like me. In this house. In this life. Because this is what they believed in. This was it for them. I knew there must be more than this and now more was rushing in to take me there. I didn't have to die, but why did Singe? Because he wanted to? Like some sort of sacrifice.

Paranoia. Stop.

Perhaps the truth was he died because he was tripping on a roof during a storm, during a robbery.

Fucking drugs again.

I wanted to spit my speeding teeth out. I felt so lonely now. Sitting alone. Speeding alone. Without Singe I'd have to go it alone. To continue the quest. To find what this 'more to life' meant for me.

More.

It got funnier every time I said it. More. More. More. And each time I said it, it meant less. Then it meant nothing. On its own, it meant zero. I spoke it out loud. It sounded even less.

"More."

I tried "to".

To was also fucked.

"Life."

I said it slowly. Like it meant something. Life had everything. So how could there be more to it?

Speed freak.

"Life. Life. Life. Life. Life."

I taunted myself. It still had everything and I had nothing.

But.

My.

Life.

So, I had... everything?

Hard to believe. Very hard. Taking-a-shit-in-the-middle-of-school-assembly hard. Impossible. Even though I remember one kid managed it in primary school. I was next to him and I saw the bulge in his grey shorts. So, not that hard.

How long before I could plug the TV in? Before I could eat. I had to do something. To take some control.

Upstairs then.

Do something. Make a choice.

Goodbye Mum and Dad. "I'm going to London. To see a band with Singe. Yes. I will be safe."

My stuff. I thought I'd need stuff. But I have nothing to take. I changed my pants and tee-shirt.

Must be love.

"I've already said goodbye to my brothers."

Lie. They're sleeping.

"I'll see the foreman when I get back."

Lie. "I love you too."

Lie? I can't tell.

My heart is beating so fast and my guts feel like they're being plaited. My lips are numb and my skin sweaty. "Yes I will. Not. No. I haven't seen him."

Goodbye Martin.

Wherever the fuck you are.

Emergency

At last I got away. To the 'phone box. To the 'phone call. The hardest thing of all. Picking up a 'phone connected to her. To someone. I smiled painfully. I don't have any money. Shit. Now it's really difficult.

Can't remember the number.

Combinations. Combinations.

Pacing, hands in pocket, my cold fingers fumble something, solid.

From the robbery.

A ten pence piece.

Shit.

What more do I need?

Calm At Sea

The morning sky was cold, dripping. Fat drizzle. My gut contracted, painful. Coming down off speed was always the worst. Depressing. Dawn had come and blurred into day. Swallowed by the hollow.

I stuck my thumb out and walked inland. Not looking back. The images of everyone, last night, watching their TVs in bright electric comfort, made my chest tighten. Like monkeys sitting, grooming, unaware of what lay across the plain, through the jungle, along the road. They sat. Comforted by the closeness. The group. We didn't want to see what was coming. Because somehow, somewhere, deep in our race memory, we knew we deserved it. We'd gotten away with it for so long. Got so far by chance and murder. We knew we had to pay. So we sat and waited. Doing everything possible to stop our eyes looking inward. Because there we'd find what we'd always known. The most terrifying thing of all.

Responsibility.

Then we'd have to do something about the shit storm advancing. No god to call out to, no aliens to rescue us. No Nirvana, no heaven, no way off the ride spinning us in our giddy little circles. No matter how many wars we fought, systems we put up, broke down. How many kings and queens we enthroned, pools coupons, spot-the-ball competitions we won, rockstars we mourned, heroes we lifted, no one could bring us safely down from this trip, but ourselves.

I cried.

For the first time since I was ten.

Tears, not for me. But for us.

I couldn't help anyone, and that would be the weight to pull me under if the sea came for me.

A knackered car pulled up, engine choking, fan belt squealing. A man with a beard and glasses wound down the window.

"Where ya going?"

"London."

"To see the Queen?"

Funny.

He opened the door.

"I can give you a lift to the motorway."

I got in and sat. The crackling radio, damp carpets, wet rust and cheap plastic seats gave me comfort.

The exhaust popped. Movement. Windscreen wipers rubbed the windscreen ineffectively, like puppy paws.

"What you doing in London?" he asked, hopefully. I hesitated, then smiled.

"Going to see a girl."

"That's nice."

"Yeah. She is."

"Hope it's drier up there."

I looked back. From the window, across the fields of cabbages, I could see the sea. Silent. Slab-like. The tide slack, blending the horizon with the drab cloud base above. Harmless now, as we rolled along the hard and fast tarmac, inland, to higher ground, away.

And all it could do was nothing. And all it could do was be there.

Waiting to turn.

For us to do something.

For us to change.

3794630R00092

Printed in Great Britain
by Amazon.co.uk, Ltd.,
Marston Gate.